I0538240

Caged

Book One of the *V to Z Trilogy*

By J.P. Robinson

ISBN-13: 978-0692792933 (Better Said Than Done)

For my family –
Of blood and water

Prologue:

Mark kept trying to change the channel when he thought Cate wasn't looking, which was most of the time, since she had a magazine in her lap while she sat taking up half the couch. Every day, after school, she put on her stupid shows that, as far as he could tell, always involved girls being mean to each other and boys not understanding what was going on, which was "very accurate," according to Cate. Cate was in middle school, after all, and Mark was still just in elementary school for another few months, so he had to trust her. If that's what middle school was like, why did she want to watch a show about what she did every day? He preferred shows with superheroes. He didn't see those every day.

Cate definitely wasn't looking. She seemed to be really into an article, probably about hair styles or something. Sensing that the moment was right, Mark slipped the remote off the table and changed to "Teen Team 6," his favorite after school show, about a group of kid superheroes who spent all their time saving the world instead of having to go to school or deal with stupid older sisters.

The show was actually on, it wasn't a commercial break, and for once he was able to watch for like five minutes solid before the channel changed.

"C'mon. I was watching that!" Mark turned to glare at his sister only to see his mom standing there, remote in hand.

She glanced down at him and said, "Sorry, sweetie. This is important."

Mom looked worried so, instead of arguing, Mark turned back to the TV. The news was on. That was even worse than Cate's shows. At least her shows weren't super boring. He didn't feel like moving though, so he'd watch for a little while, until he came up with a better idea, or dinner was ready.

The newscaster, a boring old guy in a suit, spoke in the usual oh so important newscaster voice. "We are expecting the President's address to start momentarily. And, yes, here he is now."

The boring newscaster was replaced on the screen by the President, another boring old guy. Mark looked at Cate, hoping maybe she would want to go downstairs to play foosball, but when he caught her eye, she struck him on the shoulder with her bare foot and said, "Watch. It's important."

Ha. How would she know? He turned back around anyway. Nothing better to do.

Mark had missed the start, but caught what the President said next. "In order to address the growing vampire threat, we have created a new federal agency, the National Vampire Intelligence Agency."

Mark turned to mom. "What does that mean – vampire threat?"

Cate, of course, answered first. "They're a threat cause they're monsters, stupid."

Mom said, "They're not monsters, Cate. They're humans with a blood disorder. And we don't say stupid."

Mark asked, "What's a blood disorder?"

"It's when your blood doesn't work anymore, stupid." Cate stole a quick glance at mom. "Oops, sorry. I mean, Mark."

Cate nudged his shoulder with her foot again. Why was she so annoying? Mark looked at mom, but she just continued to watch the TV, so he turned back around. The President was gone and some other guy was talking now.

"We took our first, public action last night, arresting over three hundred vees, vampires, in their lairs. Under the new law, any vampires trying to pass as human or found outside of the facilities we have created to hold them, will be considered enemies of the state and will be arrested, or terminated, if they resist arrest."

"They can't do that." Mark glanced at Mom, who stared at the TV, saying nothing more.

The TV guy said, "We ask the American people to think of the safety of our daughters and sons in helping us to locate any vees who might be hiding out in your neighborhood. A hotline has been created."

"Stupid idiots." Mom shook her head. "They can't just lock up an entire population."

Cate said, "We don't say stupid."

Mom looked for a second as if she wanted to spank Cate, but smiled wryly instead. "You're absolutely right, dear. I should have said immoral."

Mark was getting more and more confused. "What's immoral, or stupid, or whatever? Why are they idiots?"

Cate sighed loudly and then repeated, "Because you can't just lock up an entire population. Don't you know anything?"

"Cate." Mom looked at her sternly. "Your brother is not as all knowing as you, dear. He hasn't lived to be quite as mature as you."

"Nope, and he never will." Cate started to stick her foot out towards him again, but this time he dodged. If it meant he was going to be annoying and all knowing all the time, he didn't want to grow up to be as old as her!

Mom sat down on the couch next to Cate and leaned forward to put her arms around Mark. He was too old for hugs but it felt kind of nice and she let him go after a second. Mark climbed up on the couch next to her.

"Cate, I know you know all this, but for your brother's benefit I thought I would explain why I'm upset. You think you can handle listening to your much older mother for a few minutes without interrupting?"

Cate rolled her eyes and pulled her magazine back up on her lap. Mom said, "Vampires are a type of human mutant who, to survive, need to drink human blood. It's their food."

"Eww." That sounded gross.

"Yes, of course, that's what a lot of people think, it's gross. And, yes, sometimes, some vees hurt humans, or even kill them, when they are eating. They don't have to do that. Just like humans, there are good vees and bad ones."

Cate interrupted, "But humans don't eat other humans."

"That's true. Vees can't help what they are, just how they behave and some of them are trying to live peacefully, without killing for survival. This new law has basically made it illegal to be a vee. Do you see why that's wrong?"

Thinking about it that way made Mark's head hurt. "Well, they can't really do anything about it if they are already one, right?"

Mom ruffled Mark's hair and he pulled away quickly before she got the idea he enjoyed it. "You're very smart, Mark."

Cate said, "Ha," but when Mom turned to her, she had her face buried in her magazine, looking all innocent. "What?"

The TV cut back to the newscaster guy and mom went back to watching. "We have a bit more information on last night's raid. As the new Director of the NVIA stated, just over three hundred vampires were arrested across the country. The hotline number is shown below. Call if you have information that could lead to the arrest of any other vampires. To repeat what was stated earlier, vees are no longer allowed to live free in this country. We did try to locate Daniel Trevore, leader of the Vampire Liberation Front, for comment or to determine if he is still at large. Our team was unable to locate him and we have received no news of his whereabouts."

Mom turned off the TV. "I'm sure there will be more later."

She stood up and walked around the couch. "I don't feel like having pork chops for dinner after all. Would you guys be okay if I make something else and we save that for tomorrow?"

"Can we have mac n cheese?" Cate asked.

Mom said, "Sure" and started for the kitchen.

Mark thought something was more wrong than just the weird news on the TV. Mom never let them eat pasta, except on weekends. As much as he wanted to turn "Teen Team 6" back on, he wanted to make sure Mom was okay.

Following her into the kitchen, Mark said, "Mom? I'm scared."

Did he just say that? He hadn't been scared of things since he was a kid. But he realized it was true. This whole thing was scary and he didn't like it. Humans could get sick and want to eat other humans? What if he turned into a vee? What if they arrested him, or someone he knew, just because they could?

Mom crouched down so they were face to face. "I'm sorry, sweetheart. I want to tell you it will be okay, but I'm scared too."

She kissed him on the cheek and then grabbed him and pulled him in for a hug. He wanted to push her away, but it felt safe, so he hugged her back instead.

Chapter 1

The alarm sounded too soon and Cate awoke with the same thought that greeted her every morning for the past several years: "I'm still alive."

She blearily climbed out of bed and went right into the shower. Most people, she'd heard, opened the shutters as soon as they got out of bed, just to be sure. Cate thought she had more than enough nervous habits for a twenty-eight year old already. Besides, she knew it didn't matter that the sun was shining. The sun didn't mean you were safe.

It wasn't until she was nearly dressed that Cate remembered, today was the day they got the new shipment and could begin the next phase of their experiment. The thought filled her with dizzy energy. She finished dressing in a hurry, throwing on a nice pair of slacks and a blouse - she didn't do dresses - and ran out the door to get to work as early as possible.

After getting through the line of cars entering the NVIA Research Facility complex - nearly 8000 employees and only two entrances to the one garage - and all the security checkpoint crap at the main and frustratingly only entrance to the building, she hurried to her lab, as much as one could hurry while queuing up for an elevator. Once on her floor, Cate mechanically turned left, towards her end of the building, into their over large reception area. Why her team needed a reception area when no one ever visited them was beyond her. The couch and two chairs ended up being used by the scientists for lunch breaks more than anything else, even though they weren't supposed to eat "in the lab." Lisa, the admin who sat at the reception desk, was not there yet. Cate was a few minutes early, but it was odd. Lisa was almost always the first one there.

Cate passed Lisa's desk and headed down the hallway on the right. The lab area beyond was a big square, with the corridor encircling the central rooms and providing access to the offices that lined the outer wall of the building, each one coming fully decked out with a tiny slit of a window. The central rooms included the hospital rooms for patients, as well as the observation deck. The outer offices tended to be where the daily grind of scientific research and paperwork was done, as well as the storage rooms for blood and lab equipment.

Her office, the one Cate shared with the rest of her team, was a window office – something she would brag about if she had any friends, pretending the narrow slit of light that crept through could actually be considered a luxury. Since they were having a meeting this morning, Cate walked straight there, badged herself in, and nearly knocked Stan over in her charge through the door.

"Hey, slow down there cowgirl. No need to run into my arms. They're always open for you."

Stan was in his mid fifties, pale, pudgy, bald - except for what Cate liked to call his ear muffs, the little tufts of hair that grew above both ears - and the most self confident person Cate had ever met. He always treated her as if he understood she was fighting hard to keep her hands off him, and that that was okay, because he was used to the female attention.

Cate could never understand where he got all that confidence. She was in pretty good shape herself and made sure no one would ever peg her as a nerdy scientist from the way she dressed. Yet, she never felt exactly right about herself. Her nose was too big. Her smile too crooked. There was that one strand of curly hair that insisted on growing at a right angle out of the side of her head. There was always something to find wrong, some reason to not feel attractive enough. Not for Stan. He felt good all the time.

Cate pulled away from Stan. "I just didn't want to miss anything. They here yet?"

Stan smiled patiently. "How long have you worked for the government? Has anything ever arrived on time, let alone early?"

He had a point. Aside from the paperwork - my God there was a form for everything, including one to state how many forms you filled out - aside from that, the other thing Cate hated most about her job was the waiting. Requisition a new set of needles? Fine. Sure. Once the paperwork is filed, duplicated, and approved, they would place the order and then the vendor would wait to receive the inflated payment a month or two down the road before shipping, in the most economical way, the needles. It was like that with anything – supplies, policy, people.

Stan left the room, heading to his office, Cate presumed. As their boss, he actually had access to private space, though he generally spent most of his day with the team. Once Stan was gone, Cate shuffled over to her place at the bar – what they called the one long table centered in the narrow room where everyone kept their laptops - to wait. She'd come to work here because she wanted to make a difference in the world, and today could be a huge step towards that - just not yet. She turned on her computer to start work, knowing that no amount of staring at her screen would keep her settled.

While waiting for the computer to warm up, Cate opened up her lab book, reviewing the research notes she had practically memorized. The results they'd gotten were truly amazing, especially with the latest test pigs. She felt certain this vaccine would work. She barely had time to absorb any of the information in her notebook when the door opened.

She looked up hopefully, but it was just James, the newest research scientist in the team, though after two years you probably couldn't call someone new anymore. Cate had been with this group since its inception, which was only four years ago. This was her first and only job out of grad school.

James smiled when he saw her. She was sure he had a crush on her. It wasn't that he was bad looking, the opposite, in fact, but there was no way she would date anyone in the lab. For that matter, there was no way she would date anyone anymore.

"Hey Catey. How was your drive in?"

Cate had grown up in southern California, so she'd been familiar with bad traffic when she'd moved to the DC area, but she was unpleasantly surprised to find out how much commuting still sucked.

"Wonderful, as usual." Just a touch of sarcasm to start the day. "Actually, you know, 395 wasn't too bad. How about you?"

She said it before she could stop herself. Now she'd have to hear the speech.

James took on an air of superiority, that she was sure he practiced in the mirror every day, before answering, "Well, you know, that's what makes riding the bike in so great. I never get stuck in traffic. Get here a little early, shower, and good to go. I especially love it at the end of the day cause there's no one in my way."

He put down his bag and logged onto his computer.

"I'd be scared," she admitted out loud, and to herself.

"Aww, it's fine. I'm always home well before night. Besides, after today, who knows, right? Might not be a problem anymore." He smiled with his perfectly whitened teeth and she couldn't help but smile back. He was right. They were about to change the world. She hoped.

A short while of accomplishing absolutely nothing later, Stan walked back in from his office and surveyed the room. "All right, here's the update. Where's Andrew?"

As if on cue, Andrew charged into the room, knocking into Stan.

Stan looked incredulous. "What is it with you guys today? What did I do?"

Andrew grabbed a stool and sat down with a huff. "Sorry. Security caught me with a cell phone."

"Trying to send the Russians our secrets again?" James said with a laugh.

"Just forgot to leave it in the car. So, now I get to go back at the end of the day and try to find the right locker."

James rolled his eyes. "They are numbered, you know."

Cate cleared her throat, very loudly.

Andrew had the good sense to look mollified. "Right, yeah, what's up with the shipment?"

Stan sighed. "I was just about to tell you. The shipment will be here any minute. Special Agents Farino and Garmin are bringing it up now."

Cate felt a sudden lurch in her gut. "Mason Farino?"

"I don't have first names. I doubt there are a lot of Special Agent Farinos out there."

With that, Stan turned to leave, but Cate stopped him.

"I'd like to go check the hospital beds, and rooms, and make sure everything's ready."

"Good idea." With a dismissive smile, Stan walked out.

Cate looked around for her notebook, realized it was in her hand, and then knocked over a stool trying to find a pen.

"Haven't had your coffee yet?" James smiled benignly, but there was an implicit question in the way he looked at her.

He was the only man she'd ever known who actually picked up on cues – though he somehow missed the thousand and one times she told him her name was Cate, not Catey. Cate knew James was on to something. He could smell that she was nervous after hearing Mason's name and he wasn't one to drop a scent once caught. Cate didn't like opening up generally, and especially not today, and not about Mason.

"Yeah, something like that." She said, lamely.

Cate grabbed a well-gnawed pen that bore the effects of her habit and walked away before James could dig in.

The patient rooms always creeped Cate out, for no logical reason. They were perfectly sanitized, well lit, and contained all the modern instruments of any good hospital room. Still, she hated being in them. Maybe it was because she never wanted to find herself a patient here.

Instead of going directly to each room, Cate stepped into the observation deck, as they called it, to get a good view of everything. The room was a long rectangle, filled with recording devices and controls, and lined with double sided mirrors that looked into the four patient rooms. The observation deck was designed for watching and recording what was happening, without the patients knowing they were being observed. She always felt guilty watching them, even though that was part of her job.

When the pigs had been their test patients, there had just been pens in the rooms. After a thorough sanitation process, those had been replaced with hospital beds, six to each room, all equipped with ankle and wrist restraints – leather in the one room and metal in the other.

The pigs had never been there for very long. Long enough to get the injections, long enough to be tested, long enough to see if the vaccine would work. And, finally, it had. The drug had worked perfectly, and violently, and it made her sick to think about how effectively. It would all be for the best, in the end. The pigs, at least, hadn't known they were going to die. Best not to think about that. In science, sometimes you had to do things you didn't like for the greater good.

Her thoughts turned instead to the biggest mistake she'd ever enjoyed making. Mason. He wasn't the mistake. She was. If she could somehow, what, travel back in time? She shook her head, trying to dislodge unwanted musings. Today was not a day to remember regrets long buried. Today was a day to focus on the future.

Cate didn't have time to start recovering herself before the lights in one room and then another popped on, causing her to jump. Motion sensor lights were great for the environment. Not so much for her heart.

The door to room one opened up and six patients were led in. Each one quietly picked out a cot and lay down. They were so orderly; it was hard to believe they came out of a prison, although the day glo orange jump suits helped.

Getting the government to approve testing on human prisoners had been a long battle, just not one Cate had personally had to fight. As a way off death row, these men had agreed to be subjected to tests. In theory, they would survive and, eventually, be set free in gratitude for their service. In theory, the vaccine they were testing wouldn't harm them. The pigs, after all, had lived to be euthanized.

Cate was glad Stan, and probably his boss, Marisol, had been the ones to go to the meetings at Congress. She assumed the meetings were with Congressmen, but they weren't public and were above her pay grade, so who, exactly, did the approving, she wasn't sure. She was just glad they finally had humans for testing. Of course, they were only half of the shipment.

The door to room two opened and Mason Farino walked in. As he scanned the room, she watched him at work. He wasn't doing much, but he stood there very intensely. She hadn't really seen this side of him, before. He'd always been so fun, kind of goofy. She'd loved that about him. Now he looked like someone who didn't have time to smile.

His gaze swept in her direction and she blushed before remembering that he couldn't see her. Idiot. He wouldn't even know she was here. Probably wouldn't care if he did, after what she'd done to him. Her brain was leading her into dangerous territory again. This was not the time for repressed memories to surface. And then she saw the second half of the shipment, and Mason Farino wasn't so important anymore.

Four armed guards escorted them in, with two guards posted at the door. Each one was manacled to the next, but unlike the other prisoners, they were in street clothes. Mason chained them one by one to their own cots. There were only four, Cate noticed. That was okay. Really, it only took one dead vampire to find out if the vaccine worked, and now they had four.

Chapter 2

Mason stood waiting for Frank in the garage. He'd driven to work, logged in, got his coffee, and been given the assignment to leave headquarters immediately and drive to the National Vampire Intelligence Agency research facility all while Frank apparently figured out today was a work day.

When Mason called Frank to let him know they had to leave, Frank said he was "parking the car." That had been fifteen minutes ago and Mason was just now watching as Frank drove up.

He stopped the car next to Mason and rolled the passenger side window down. "What? Traffic was awful."

Mason got in next to his partner. "Traffic is always awful. Somehow the rest of us get here on time."

Frank started driving. The NVIA headquarters, where Mason and Frank reported every day, was in Arlington, Virginia. It was just another office building, so far as everyone in the area knew. At least, that was the idea. In reality, everyone in the area probably knew, if not exactly what type of agency was there, at least that it was a federal agency.

For some reason, maybe due to the scope, the NVIA research facility had been built in the suburbs of Oakton. The area had townhouses, single family homes, shops, and a large wooded area with a secure medical campus hidden within. Again, residents could probably guess at some of what happened there. Officially, though, it was just another building.

"This sucks." Frank honked his horn for emphasis. "You know, two weeks ago I was in Ireland?"

It was too early for this. "Don't start on that again."

"You know what they got there? Rolling green hills, castles around every corner, and great beer."

Mason rolled his eyes. "Yeah, you know, I heard. Like forty-six times since you got back from your honeymoon. Can we not talk about it for maybe an hour?"

"Yeah, well, it's not like you have a life. What are we supposed to talk about?"

Frank had a way of making Mason feel like crap without even trying.

"Why don't we talk about the job? Maybe figure out the day?"

"What's there to figure out? We sign in, pick up some vees from the basement, escort them upstairs, and leave. Then we go home, right?"

In a nutshell, yeah, that about summed it up. Of course, nothing was ever that simple at the NVIA.

Upon arriving, he and Frank signed themselves and the car in through the main gate onto campus. To enter the building, they had to leave their cell phones, tablets, jump drives, and anything else with any kind of signaling or storage capability behind. As Special Agents, however, they were allowed to bring in their guns.

After showing their IDs to the camera, they entered the building one at a time. Mason stepped through the first bullet proof glass door, waited for it to close, and then heard the slight whirring sound as he was scanned for devices. Once all clear, the inner bullet proof glass door opened and he was allowed to step into the vast, bland lobby where a guard scanned him again. Frank followed behind and they were issued visitor badges and a temporary escort who would lead them downstairs.

"Why so quiet?" Frank asked as they walked down the stairs towards Security Central Control.

Mason didn't answer. Frank knew he hated this place. Most of what happened here was above his clearance, so Mason didn't exactly know what went on. He could guess. He'd delivered plenty of vee prisoners to this building. He'd never once taken a vee out of the building.

Frank rolled his eyes at Mason's non responsiveness. "Aww, c'mon. You're not starting to feel all dirty again, are you? I thought we went over this?"

"Shut up, Frank." His partner really didn't know when to stop sometimes.

Frank said, "Today's a cakewalk. Before you know it, I'll be home with the wife and you'll be, well, you'll be home."

Frank loved pushing Mason's buttons. His winning personality was what made him the world's most endearing partner. Mason tried to ignore him, and the dig – one of many he had to suffer daily – at his bachelor status.

Frank continued philosophically, "You gotta take the easy assignments with the fun ones. Can't be walking into a vee hive every day, can we?"

If Mason bothered to look at him, Frank would probably wink, and then Mason would have to shoot him, so he just kept staring straight ahead until they got to SCC.

Annoyingly, every time they came to the research facility - which, thankfully, was only twice a year or so - they had to report in to SCC for a green visitor badge and an SCC assigned escort. Mason loathed the inefficiency of it almost as much as he hated the irrationality. The security guards here weren't field agents. They were facility security guards. Yet he and Frank had to be escorted by them to and from the vee prison as if they couldn't be trusted to be left on their own, which was absurd, considering every time a vee was transported, a Special Agent was required to be present.

SCC was a split level, open space office filled with long desks with several computers on each, a wall of storage that Mason assumed held weapons, as well as one wall devoted to security camera monitors constantly cycling. A few guards sat at computers, a couple watched the wall of monitors and several looked like they were just hanging out in a little seating area. Mason and Frank were handed off to a guard who sat at the desk near the all important badge printer. Frank, knowing Mason's mood, handled most of the paperwork. Mason still had to show his ID again and sign in. Mason and Frank were issued one walkie to use while on site, which Frank handed to him. They were also given their green badges, which were about as useless as the red ones. He could badge himself into the bathroom, but not much else.

"Althea." The badge printing guard called out, and a young woman who'd been hanging out in the seated area, walked over. "You're up."

She was wearing the black mock turtleneck armor all the guards wore, under her gray uniform. Mason thought the armor was ridiculous. The turtleneck portion wasn't bullet proof or even bite proof. It might slow a vee down, if he was going straight for the neck. A vee trying to escape this facility would probably be trying to kill and not feed anyway, and the uniforms left plenty of other vulnerable places open to attack.

Mason stepped forward to make introductions. "I'm Special Agent Farino and this is Special Agent Garmin."

She looked Mason up and down, smirked, and then nodded at Frank. "Yeah, you can just call me Althea."

Frank nudged Mason, and gave him a look that said, "Now don't you feel like an ass," as they followed Althea out into the corridor.

The vee prison, as it was referred to verbally, never in writing, was just down the hall from SCC. Mason had never needed to go past the guard station to drop off or receive prisoners - the vees he transported were taken from him or delivered to him outside the prison door checkpoint – still, he knew that there were fifty holding cells built into a sub basement facility beneath where they were standing.

As they approached the prison door, they saw six human prisoners, in the orange day glo uniforms of an actual state prison, lined up against the wall, with four security guards watching them. Mason assumed, by the clothes, that these were the death row prisoners who were also being taken to the labs.

Althea looked back at Mason and Frank and nodded towards the human prisoners, "You got an extra big load today."

Frank laughed. Mason just shook his head.

Escorting vees through a building while being escorted themselves was ridiculous. Add in transporting human prisoners, who were surrounded by armed guards, and the day became surreal.

After signing more papers and showing more ID, they received four male vee prisoners. The only thing that distinguished the vee prisoners from the human prisoners was that they were in street clothes, since they weren't officially prisoners given that, officially, the prison didn't exist.

As for biologically visible distinctions between human and vee, there weren't any. Vees looked human. As someone who spent a lot of time around vees, Mason could sometimes pick a vee out of a crowd by the way they moved. Vees were inherently stronger and faster than humans, and occasionally one would move too quickly or pick something heavy up too easily. To an unpracticed eye, the differences were nearly impossible to detect.

After checking the restraints, Mason turned to Althea. "Would you like to lead the way?"

She smiled and started walking towards the stairs. With all the prisoners and guards, the elevators would've been inconvenient, not to mention unsafe. The building was eight stories high and they were in the basement, so Mason was happy they were only going to the fifth floor.

Frank fell in beside Althea and started telling her about Ireland. Mason easily tuned him out. He wished he could as easily ignore his own thoughts. He hated the bureaucracy of the NVIA. There was so much waste. Coming here to act as babysitters, when the guards onsite could clearly handle taking the vees for a walk, was just one of many stupid policies Mason had to deal with.

He'd become an agent, a field agent, because he wanted to protect people. As altruistic as it sounded, Mason had really wanted to help make America safe again. Unfortunately, he spent half of his days performing dumb jobs that anyone could do – and this was one of those days.

What made today worse was that Mason was certain there were things going on in this facility that his stomach didn't agree with.

He understood the need to find a cure, the need to stop vampirism from spreading. He knew that figuring out how to do that required testing. He also knew that not every vee he arrested was evil, not every vee he arrested was even a killer. Many of them had found ways to live with human donors. Some of them had even returned to their families, after the change, hiding in secret rooms by day, tucking their kids in at night. Yet Mason was to arrest them, just the same, and take them to places where they disappeared, places like this.

Mason had learned, after his first few months at the agency, that it was best to put such thoughts out of his head, as much as possible. Frank was the most tolerant special agent Mason had discussed the idea of innocent vees with, the idea that biological testing on unwilling subjects was unethical. Frank was tolerant because he didn't tell Mason he was an idiot, or a vee sympathizer, or threaten to report him. He'd just told him to shut up.

On the fifth floor, Frank stood guard in the hallway while Mason inspected the vee lab room. It looked like a hospital room, except the cots had restraints on them, and there was a wall to wall mirror on the far side of the room. He wondered, as one did when looking at a two way mirror, if someone was watching him.

The guards led the vees in and strapped them down by their wrists. Mason went from one to the next, to the next, checking that the restraints were secured. The first two lay quietly while Mason looked over their restraints. The short, chubby one with the peace tee shirt and hoodie actually pulled at his chains like he was trying to break free.

The last vee he checked was tall, thin, and had piercing blue eyes that seemed to take everything in. Mason recognized him. It'd been a long time since he'd seen him on the news, but this was the guy who'd been trying to get vees the right to vote. As Mason bent over him, the vee very loudly sniffed him.

Mason startled. A knee-jerk reaction to an unexpected sound. The vee smiled. He was trying to assert control, to show that he wasn't afraid. Mason felt bad for him. He still thought he had the power to scare someone. Mason was sure that, before the night was out, the vee would be the one who was scared.

Chapter 3

Daniel surveyed his new surroundings from the hospital bed. They weren't bad, for a prison, or a lab, as he understood this place to be. The bed had clean linens on it, which was odd considering what they planned to do him and the other vees in this room, as if providing this one small comfort in some way compensated for taking away their freedom and very likely their lives. Not that he planned to stick around long enough to find out exactly what they would do, if he let them.

The two way mirror was a bit of a joke. Did they think vees were brain dead animals incapable of reason? A lot of people seemed to think the opposite, that vampires had magical qualities - like seeing through two way mirrors, perhaps, or having no reflection. The truth was a bit less exciting. Daniel couldn't fly, change into a bat, or control minds. He could see himself in the mirror as often as he wanted to, and, let's be honest, he often wanted to. Not at the moment, of course. He hadn't showered in nearly a week. So he didn't strain to see himself in the mirror, nor did he try to peer through it, since both would be a waste of time.

The agent guy, the one who looked too skinny to be a cop, checked the chains on each of the vees before heading for the door. Daniel made sure to smell him, loudly, when he leaned over his bed. Daniel loved smelling humans. For one thing, it freaked them out. For another, you could always get a sense of who the person was from how they smelled. That was one thing vees all had in common, heightened senses.

There was nothing special about this cop. There rarely was. The liked coffee and curry and washed with some generic brand of soap. Thankfully, he did not employ after shave. Sometimes sniffing could backfire and send you into a sneezing fit. It's very hard to appear threatening whilst sneezing. Daniel kept cool, sniffed loudly, and startled the guy, giving Daniel a moment to treasure. Sure, it was childish, but you had to get your kicks where you could find 'em in a place like this.

As soon as the agents had left and closed the door, Carl started talking. Daniel had come to realize that talking was this Carl's "thing." Carl was short, pudgy, and pale and he talked nonstop. More specifically, he plotted nonstop. Carl's magical vampire power seemed to be never getting tired of hearing his own theories.

"What do you think these chains are made of? There's probably something in this room we can use. Look around you guys. I'm sure we can find a stick or something."

"A stick? A stick? What the heck do you think you're gonna accomplish with a stick?"

That was Jerome piping up. Jerome was the opposite of Carl. Tall, dark, and built like a wrecking ball, with about the same amount of patience. Daniel just ignored Carl, and the rest of them for that matter. Jerome couldn't bear Carl's stupidity. He kept trying to find a way to fix him.

"First of all, a stick would just break, you try to put that up against metal." Jerome argued. "Secondly, you think we're gonna find a key or a crowbar lying around? Is that what you think? Cause I am pretty sure they thought of that when they brought us in here."

Carl cried, "Well, I don't know! All I'm saying is we need to look around, figure out some options."

Daniel tuned out the rest of the conversation. He'd only been in the cells with these guys, and the other vees who hadn't been brought up to this room, for a week. One week since he'd been imprisoned. Time for a change.

The guards had let him and the other vees keep their own clothes, though they took away belts and anything shiny. They didn't take his shoe laces though. Guess they weren't afraid of suicides, which was a mistake, considering how ratty he felt in week old clothes. Fortunately, vees didn't have much body odor, so the clothes didn't stink or anything, but he was missing his fresh scented, clean wardrobe all the same.

Daniel hadn't been looking to make friends in here. He tried to keep to himself. Having a reputation that preceded him made that difficult.

"Hey, terrorist vee." This nickname was one of Carl's gems.

"I know you can hear me. You got a plan or something? You got a way out from some of your secret military friends?"

Daniel sat up, as much as the restraints allowed, and fixed Carl a stare that would shut up a smarter vee.

"I know you know something." Carl gloated, definitely not taking the hint. "Yeah, you got something planned. You gonna share?"

"I have told you before, I am not a terrorist. I prefer to think of myself as a pacifist." Daniel smiled as if to imply that he'd rip Carl's throat out if Carl tried to disagree.

"Would you leave the vee alone?" Jerome said. "Who gives a shit if he blows up buildings? He's in here same as us and he's screwed same as us."

That wasn't quite true. Daniel did have a plan, though the losers sharing this cell didn't need to know that. So far, everything was going swimmingly. The hard part was the waiting, especially with the way Carl was acting.

The fourth roommate was quiet. Daniel had always been partial to the quiet ones. He'd been quiet himself, when he was younger. The problem with the quiet ones is you couldn't read them. Daniel *knew* Jerome. It had taken about five minutes to figure him out. He was a survivor, who would do what it took, but wasn't one for leading or forging new paths.

The quiet one, Stephen, he was still a wild card. Not that Daniel was planning on having to deal with him for very long, but you never knew how it would all play out, until the game was done, and Daniel preferred to know what cards everyone was holding.

Daniel had always been good at planning, always been good at knowing which way the wind would blow. He was sure this little scheme would hold no surprises. Very few things surprised him anymore. In the 80 years he'd been alive, he'd grown almost bored.

Daniel had been a 30-year-old, WASPy accountant when he was turned. Vampires were still mostly unknown at the time, at least as things of reality. He hadn't asked to be turned, but he hadn't fought very hard either.

Kenneth, his maker, hadn't seduced Daniel in the traditional way. Daniel had always been partial to females. Kenneth had offered him something he'd never found in his life – adventure; the chance to be a completely different person, a completely different thing. That was what he'd wanted more than anything. Of course, fifty years later, it was hard to feel like anything was an adventure anymore, and he hadn't really ever become completely different. He was still himself, just with a new set of biological rules. He even looked much the same. In the past 50 years, he'd only aged, physically, about ten.

The silence caught his attention and he looked around to see everyone watching the door. Daniel hadn't heard the key, too lost in his thoughts, but he was at full attention now. This was important. This was the enemy. He needed to know them, and quickly.

Two people in lab coats entered the room, one male, one female. There were security guards with them, of course, but they weren't important. Guards everywhere were all the same – incapable of thinking for themselves. Scientists, on the other hand, were very capable of thinking up new ways to destroy. The male looked like he grew his own pot and only ate organic. He also looked nervous, even if he spoke to them in a soothing manner, like they were a room of school children.

"We just need a sample of your blood for testing. This will only take a minute." The male headed over to Jerome first. The guards held Jerome down while the man took his sample. Jerome didn't fight, there was no reason. Carl, on the other hand, was working himself up.

"When you gonna feed us? It's been days. You can't starve us to death. We need some blood here."

The male tried to calm him. Daniel ignored them and observed the woman. As the guards held Stephen down, and the woman drew his blood, Stephen seemed to watch her, silently, with great interest. She barely glanced at him, and seemed to nestle as close to the guard next to her as possible, as if his body heat could keep her safe.

Daniel thought, against his better judgment, that she was beautiful, despite the frizzy hair. She had that ageless quality to her that some women had, where you couldn't tell if she was 22 or 42. She was less nervous than the male scientist. There was something else there, something in the way she kept her eyes down. Not fear, more like guilt. He felt almost sorry for her, as today was not going to work out well for her, or any of her colleagues. Not sorry enough to change his plans, though.

And then she was standing beside him, preparing the needle. As she leaned in to take his blood, Daniel inhaled her. It had been a long time since he'd found himself unable to contain a smile. She looked at him, worriedly, as he grinned and grinned. When she walked out the door, Daniel kept smiling. It had been too long since anything had surprised him. Daniel smiled and smiled, remembering, once again, what it felt like to be utterly surprised.

Chapter 4

Cate didn't like the way that that one vampire had smelled her. She shouldn't have let herself get so close to him, should've kept the guard between them. She was sure he knew. With any luck he'd be dead before he tried to say anything. That would wipe that creepy smile off his face.

Cate immediately regretted the thought. She shuddered to think about killing them. The last time round they'd only had one to test on. Even though this was why she came to work for the NVIA instead of the many, better paying, labs who'd offered her jobs, she'd still been shaken when they'd killed him.

His name had been Hank. She didn't talk to him much, just enough to know he had thoughts, feelings, an expectation of a life to live. When they brought him in the room with the vaccinated pigs, he refused. Even though he must've been starving by that point, he wouldn't touch them. She'd expected that. They'd all expected that. In her mind, that was the result, the proof they needed. When Hank was back in his room, she assured him they would feed him soon, and had meant it.

Of course, she'd been wrong. Stan had James give Hank the injection of vaccinated blood. Cate felt like protesting, injecting him was unnecessary, but that wasn't true. Cate thought she should've fought for the right to do the injection herself, shown she had the strength to do it. She'd known she didn't. She didn't have the stomach for it, even if that was part of her job.

Hank did not die quickly. They watched from the observation deck as he screamed and screamed. She would never forget that sound. It was the second most horrible thing she'd ever heard. And, if everything went the way it was supposed to, they were going to do worse to these four. Since they couldn't very well go around injecting every vee out there in the real world, they needed to know how the blood interacted with vees who'd bitten a vaccinated human. Like Hank, they would refuse to feed. Unlike Hank, they wouldn't have a choice. The guards would force feed them. Cate didn't have the stomach to watch that, either.

This was what she wanted. If the vaccine worked, vampires would no longer be able to feed on humans. They would find another food source or go extinct trying. It would all be for the good. Still, she wouldn't talk to them this time. She wouldn't make the mistake of knowing anything about them again.

After Cate put her vee blood samples into storage, she and Andrew headed back towards the office. Cate let Andrew get ahead of her when she saw Lisa, her one good work friend, walking down the hall.

Lisa looked like she'd just arrived, still carrying her bag, which would make her very late. Lisa wasn't the type of person who was ever late, and she looked like she'd had a rough morning already. Of course, being nearly nine months pregnant, Cate was sure most of Lisa's mornings were rough.

"Have a doctor's appointment this morning?"

Lisa nearly jumped out of her skin, obviously having not noticed Cate yet.

"You gave me a heart attack!" Lisa took a deep breath. "Don't go sneaking up on me like that."

"Got it." Cate responded, wryly. "I will no longer deploy stealth mode when walking directly up to you."

Lisa gave Cate the kind of smile that showed she hadn't been listening. In fact, she looked like she had better things to be doing.

"So, should I let you get back to work?" Cate had things to do as well.

Lisa replied as if surprised to be in a conversation. "What? Oh, yeah. Yeah, I have lots of paperwork I gotta catch up on." She looked longingly towards her desk.

Cate wanted to ask her more, see if she wanted to talk about it, but she did have to get back to work. There was a lot to get done, before the waiting started.

"Talk to you later?" Cate squeezed Lisa's arm.

Lisa hugged her, pulled away and didn't wait for any more questions before walking off down the hall. Cate would have to find out what that was about later.

Everyone was in the office when Cate walked in. Stan looked ready to give a speech, so Cate just grabbed a stool and sat down.

"In the pigs, this vaccine took a little over four hours. Could be the same, longer, or shorter on our human prisoners. Now we just wait."

Cate was taken off guard. "I'm sorry, I must've missed something. Did you already vaccinate the prisoners?"

"Yes. I saw no reason to wait after we collected their baseline. I assisted James in administering the vaccine."

"Don't you think we would've all liked to have been there? What about the director? She specifically…"

Stan cut her off. "Marisol," he said, as if the name carried no weight with him, "specifically requested we let her office know, which I did. And no, I didn't think you'd need to see a bunch of prisoners be given shots. If it makes you feel better, you can be there when they feed the vees, assuming that becomes necessary."

Cate suspected Stan knew how much she didn't want to be there for that. For some reason, there was a power play going on around her and she couldn't make heads or tails of it. At least, not quickly enough to come up with a satisfactory response.

Stan eyed her for a second, making sure she wasn't about to interrupt again, and then continued. "On that note, as anticipated, we should prepare to be here after dark. I guess I'll just ask, is there anyone who has a problem staying the night?"

Chapter 5

Standing in the hall outside the lab while Frank shot the shit with the guards, Mason saw a ghost. As she walked away down the hall, turning into an office, he caught the merest glimpse of her profile. He knew it was her. She looked exactly like he remembered her.

More than 8000 people worked at the NVIA research facility on any given day. Mason had never suspected Cate was one of them. He'd purposely not looked her up over the years - better for him if he didn't know where she was, if he couldn't picture her today. Of course, he'd pictured her anyway, but never, once, had that picture involved her working for the agency.

In college she'd been active in the vee integration movement. She'd dragged him into it, briefly. Protesting for legal rights for vees. She used to say that they were just like us, with a slight biological change.

That was not the belief commonly held at the NVIA. From what he knew of the NVIA labs, it was certainly not the belief of her department. In school, Mason had held Cate while she cried over having to run experiments on rats. Cate working here made no sense.

"Ready?" Frank was nudging him.

"What?" For a moment, Mason, lost in his past, couldn't figure out why Frank was there.

"Ready to go sign out? I know you want to stay here all day, but I got a comfy desk to sit behind back at the office."

Althea was waiting to escort them back to SCC. Frank looked about ready to nudge him again.

"Uh, yeah. Sure." Mason muttered.

Lost in thought while they descended the gray concrete stairwell and walked down the seemingly endless, drab, basement corridor, they were almost to the door to SCC before Mason figured out what he wanted to say.

"Actually, before we go in there," Mason said.

Frank and Althea stopped walking and looked at him expectantly. Mason turned to Althea, avoiding Frank's stare.

"If I wanted to look someone up, is there a computer I could use? And someone who could give me access?"

"I could do that." Althea offered. "If this is official business, of course, anyone in security could help."

"Let's just keep this between us for now," Mason said.

To her credit, Althea didn't react at all. Frank just raised an eyebrow, in silent question. Mason shook his head. He didn't have an answer.

"What kind of access do you need?" Althea asked. "We can access a lot more in SCC, but if you just need general database stuff, we can go to the lab."

Mason shrugged. "I just need to look someone up in the register."

"Cool. Follow me, gentlemen." As Althea headed down the hall away from SCC, she yelled back over her shoulder. "You get to keep those shiny badges for a little longer."

The lab was a small office, undecorated and empty except for the six cheap desks, folding chairs, and desktop computers that looked like they'd been resuscitated from the junk heap. One computer was occupied by a guard playing solitaire.

"Joe." Althea nodded towards him.

Joe, glancing up, smiled back. "Hey."

Althea jerked her head towards Mason and Frank and Joe nodded knowingly. He took about two seconds to wrap up his game before standing up. He said, "Later," and left them alone in there.

"You guys overwhelmed with work?" Frank joked.

"End of day." Althea explained. "Not much going on between now and the night shift taking over."

Althea sat down at a computer and logged in while Frank and Mason pulled up chairs.

With her password entered, the home screen blinked on. Mason reached for the mouse. "May I?"

Althea pulled it away, protectively. "No, you may not."

Mason considered trying to pull rank. Ultimately, he didn't need to drive anyway, so he raised his hands in surrender.

"Who do you want to look up?" Althea asked.

When something looked out of place, it usually was. Mason was in the habit of finding out why. "Any chance we could look up the vees we just transferred?"

Frank asked, "What's up?"

Althea pulled up a log sheet and Mason leaned in to read.

"Daniel Trevore! Remember him?" Mason asked.

Frank shook his head. "Should I?"

Althea said, "No way."

Mason smiled, wryly. "Weird, right?"

Frank looked at them both as if they were crazy. "What am I missing here?"

"You know the Vee Liberation Front? Daniel Trevore is the guy started it all, way back in the day," Mason explained.

"He went missing around the time the NVIA was created," Althea added. "Haven't heard anything about him for at least ten years."

"Aaand?" Frank asked.

"Aaand, we just transferred him upstairs." Mason sat back in his chair, as if that was all he had to say, but Frank was being dense for some reason.

Frank asked, "So? We got him. Yay?"

"Isn't it kind of weird that the face of the vee liberation movement, the most famous vee our country has ever had, someone who's been missing from the public and who we haven't apprehended in 15 years at least, suddenly turns up here, and it's no big deal?"

"How could they have booked him into the prison under his own name with no one noticing?" Althea asked.

That bothered Mason too. Someone like Daniel Trevore would have an alias, or four. Why hadn't he used one of those? And, failing to do that, why had no one suspected anything when his name came up? His name would've been flagged, without a doubt.

Mason shrugged. "I don't know. Is there someone we could ask?"

Althea deflated. "Yeah. That would be my boss."

Mason wanted to go there about as much as Althea did. Maybe, when he had more than a suspicion, maybe then he'd work his way up the ranks, risking his own. For now, there were a few more lines of investigation open.

"We can hold off on that," Mason said. Althea looked understandably relieved. "Let's see what's in that computer, what would've come up for the guards signing him in. And when we're done, we can go ask Mr. Trevore what he was thinking."

"So," said Frank, realization dawning, "what you're saying is, you don't want to go back to HQ after all?"

Mason smiled. He loved the moment when you knew you'd caught the scent. He wasn't sure what it was yet, but he knew it smelled.

Chapter 6

Cate stood alone on the observation deck. Andrew, who would be her teammate for the night, had had to hang behind to confirm his dog sitter so, for the second time today, she found herself alone in that room. This time, at least, there was something to see.

The prisoners, the human prisoners, unlike the vees, were not restrained. Cate assumed that was because they were all volunteers. Still, no one entered the room without the armed guards, volunteers or not. Stan and James had no problem drawing blood samples and left when they were done. The guards closed the doors behind them and the prisoners went back to biding their time, something Cate assumed they all had a lot of practice at. They'd given them books, playing cards and magazines, since there was no TV. Two of the prisoners were reading. One was sleeping, but snoring loudly enough that Cate could tell he was breathing. The other three were sitting up on their cots complaining to each other while they played poker. Apparently, they weren't happy with the way they'd been treated since being released from death row. Strange to think these men had done something to end up on death row. Strange to think they would be free soon, despite their crimes, and would be safer going about their business than most humans, if the vaccine did work.

Cate doubted there would be any external signs of changes to their system. The pigs had become first lethargic and then agitated, but other than that had seemed to continue with normal pig behavior. Stan's plan to have two teams rotating between the observation deck and the lab was really a way to keep the two scientists who weren't running tests occupied, if watching a bunch of men sit around in a locked room could be called an occupation.

The pigs that they'd injected with the vaccine had been put down shortly after having served their purpose. They hadn't yet studied the long term effect of the drug, the effect on subsequent generations, or how the vaccinated blood changed, if at all, from subject to subject or with different modes of introduction. In a rare case of rapid speedy approval, their team was being allowed to use humans as guinea pigs well before they'd exhausted all forms of testing on actual pigs. Cate did not have enough empirical evidence to know just how things would develop over time, or tonight, for that matter.

The human subjects were to be observed for at least a month, assuming the vaccine had the desired initial effect. They needed to study the vaccinated patients for a period of time, before the vaccine could be introduced into the main population, to make sure the effects of the drug persisted.

Cate turned to look at the vees. Two of them were having what seemed to be an old argument while the other two, including that one with the know-it-all smile, sat quietly staring at the ceiling. Almost as if he could feel her watching him, he turned in his bed and looked right through her. The other, quiet one, followed suit. She broke out in goosebumps.

"That's freaky." Andrew said, almost in Cate's ear. He'd somehow managed to walk right up behind her without her noticing. "It's like they're staring right at us."

"They smelled you." Cate sighed.

"You saying I smell?" Andrew grumbled, acting hurt. "That's not nice."

Cate laughed. He did smell, like patchouli, but that wasn't what she'd meant. "Well, either that or they heard you. I'm pretty sure this glass is sound proof and they tend to have a stronger sense of smell than anything else. At least, some of them do. Just like humans, you know, some have better senses than others."

Andrew said, "Yeah, just like humans - smelling through bullet proof glass."

Cate grinned. Out of everyone on the team, she liked Andrew the best. Unlike Cate, he wasn't afraid to be himself. And unlike Stan and James, he seemed to be here for the science, more than for the career.

Andrew spent the hour regaling Cate with stories of his dog, Rex, the golden retriever, and his cell phone, the smartest of smart phones. By the end of the hour, she wasn't sure which one he cared about more. She was certain she didn't want to ask to find out.

At the turn of their shift, she and Andrew drew a sample of blood from each of the six human prisoners. The guards stood in the room with them, looking threatening. None of the prisoners so much as made a nasty comment.

Cate was fairly certain there would be nothing special in the blood, yet. She agreed with Stan's approach - checking the blood on an hourly basis was good research – it just meant a lot of dull work.

They ran the tests, took notes, and hardly talked at all, which was a relief. Andrew was nice. Unlike Stan and James, he treated her like an equal. But after just an hour trapped in that room together, Cate felt like she knew more than she ever wanted to know about him already.

When they had run every test and recorded the data - predictably, finding no change - they packed up the samples. As they stepped out into the hallway, Cate came face to face with Director LaTrese.

Marisol LaTrese had the unenviable job of managing all the scientific research at NVIA. She rarely showed herself at any of the labs. Cate wasn't surprised she'd made an appearance today. Today was, potentially, an historic day.

Marisol didn't look happy. "I'm here to see Stan." She began to pass Cate and Andrew, heading towards his office. Andrew stopped her.

"He's not here."

Marisol turned on him. "He's not here? Today?"

Cate interjected. "He's on the observation deck. We're heading there now."

Marisol fell in next to them as they walked.

"You administered the vaccine then?" Marisol asked.

Cate replied, "Yes. We're just waiting on the results."

"I see." Marisol's lips couldn't get any tighter.

Cate looked at Andrew for a clue. He just shrugged, so they walked the rest of the way in silence.

When Stan opened the door to the room, Marisol pushed her way in, gestured for James to leave, and then closed the door behind them.

"That was exciting." James looked at the two of them. "Any idea what that was about?"

Before Cate could respond that, no, she had no idea, the door opened and Marisol walked away without saying another word. Stan stepped out.

"It's all yours." Stan gestured to the room as if nothing had just happened.

"Anything wrong?" Cate asked.

"We'll talk about that later." Stand answered, dismissively. "We have blood to test."

After making sure nothing, in fact, was visibly happening with the prisoners, Andrew asked, "What the hell was that about?"

"I'm guessing Stan's in trouble. I'm not sure why." She had her suspicions. Better not to voice those things out loud at the NVIA.

"Maybe he didn't let her know that we were proceeding with the injections." Andrew offered.

"Yeah, I guess." Cate agreed, despite thinking that it must've been something worse than that for Marisol to confront him face to face, without scheduling an official interview. Very unbureaucratic of her! "I guess we'll find out, right? Stan'll tell us?"

Andrew just shrugged and then stood staring at the prisoners. He stayed silent, leaving Cate some time to think. Andrew never liked to say anything negative about anyone, one of his better qualities. Cate guessed his silence was answer enough. Stan didn't have to tell them anything he didn't want to, and, lately, there seemed to be a lot of things he wasn't sharing with her, or Andrew.

The politics didn't matter. They were about to make history, all of them, even if Stan's name was the one that got recorded in the books. Cate was just happy she got to be a part of work that would make such a huge difference in the world.

As slow as the government was in every other way, they moved fast on vee research. The NVIA had been able to make human subjects available in record speed. If this worked, they could be mass producing within the year. And then everything would change, for the world, and for her.

There was no visible change over the next hour, however, so she and Andrew got ready to draw more blood. As they walked past the guards posted outside the vees' room, Cate felt bad for them. These guards were going to be stuck here all night, staring at an ugly wall, with absolutely nothing to occupy them. At least the guards outside the human prisoner's room got to unlock and lock the door every hour.

As they approached, Cate smiled at the guards who would be letting her and Andrew in to the room. One of them hardly glanced back, but the other one smiled and arched an eyebrow, as he took out his keys. "Ready for some excitement?"

Cate nodded. "Always."

As soon as the door opened, the jovial mood disintegrated. Cate was suddenly glad there were two guards with her.

Seemingly nothing had changed. The prisoners were all alive. They weren't acting out or yelling - just the opposite. The room was eerily quiet.

The two guards stood at the door as Andrew entered first. Cate followed, pushing the sample tray in. She could feel that something was wrong. In addition to the silence, there was a smell. It smelled like a nursing home, not like a group of young, healthy men.

Most of the prisoners were lying down. One was standing by his bed, staring at them. He looked like he was asleep on his feet, except that his gaze followed Andrew.

Andrew took a needle. "Guess I'll start with him."

As Andrew approached the prisoner, Cate was hit with a sinking feeling. For a split second, she thought to stop him, pull him back. She dismissed the feeling as irrational. There was no good reason to stop him, or so it seemed, for that one second.

And then Andrew was screaming. And blood was staining his lab coat.

The prisoner was holding Andrew tightly and ripping off chunks of his shoulder and neck with his teeth. Without thought, Cate ran up to them and pushed her way between them. She shoved the prisoner back. He seemed stunned, like he hadn't realized what was happening.

Cate grabbed Andrew, practically picking him up, and carried him out into the hallway, dropping him to the floor. The guards, guns drawn now, retreated with them. Cate turned back towards the lab, putting herself defensively between Andrew and the door. The friendly guard started to pull the door closed. Cate saw the prisoner, the one with blood around his mouth, seem to come to his senses and start to charge. The guard pulled the door closed just as the prisoner crashed into it.

The mindless violence of what had just happened shook her, but what scared her more was what she saw just before the door closed. All the prisoners were sitting up in their beds, and every one of them was staring at her, or rather, it seemed, at the blood on her shirt.

Chapter 7

Daniel could smell the blood. They all could. At any other time, especially when he was starving, the aroma would be intoxicating. But there was a different odor that was overpowering, and it killed any appetite he might've had.

Carl had started pulling at his restraints and shouting. "When are they gonna let us out? You gotta let us out of here. Anyone hear me?!"

Jerome just kept repeating, "Shut up. Shut the fuck up." Repeating it like a chant, like it would soothe him.

Then the alarm sounded. Most office buildings built in the last ten years or so came with a daylight alarm system. Daniel hadn't worked in an office building for a very long time. Still, he knew they generally sounded an hour before sundown, and then again every fifteen minutes until what was usually lockdown time for most buildings. Daniel had been keeping track and knew this was the thirty minute warning. Half an hour until the sun went down. He could almost feel the night in his bones.

When the alarm died, Stephen broke his silence. "You aren't as calm anymore."

Stephen was talking to him, and Daniel knew he was right, but he didn't like being the subject of his attention.

"I'm always calm." Daniel retorted.

Carl stopped yelling. Subsequently, Jerome's chanting ceased. They both turned their attention to him and Stephen, as if this conversation was a diversion from the fear that had begun to seep into the room.

"Cause you always have a plan?" Daniel heard the derision in Stephen's voice. "How's that working out for you now?"

Carl piped up. "That's right. You have a plan. When we getting out?"

Daniel snapped back, "I don't have a plan. I never claimed to have one. Go back to panicking and leave me alone."

That should shut him up, at least, for a few seconds. Daniel needed time to think. This new situation with whatever was next door hadn't been part of the plan. It really shouldn't change anything, at least, not so far as his night was concerned. However, there might be a way to improve the situation, if the timing worked out how he hoped it would.

Depending on how long she took, things might be absolutely...

He heard the door being unlocked.

"Perfect."

As Carl started whining again, Daniel allowed himself to smile.

A guard walked in, looked around, stationed himself by the door. Daniel noticed that there was only one guard – he'd expected two – and that the guard was agitated.

Lisa entered the room, dressed in a lab coat that wouldn't close over her enormous belly, and pushing a phlebotomy cart. She smiled at the guard while he closed the door behind her. She looked so calm and innocent, though Daniel could smell her fear.

Lisa said, "I'm so sorry about this."

"Just make it quick." The guard didn't exactly point to what was going on down the hall, but his body language read, "I want to get in on the action."

"I'll just be a second." She did a kind of guilt riddled smile and the guard smiled back. Human males never could doubt the word of a pregnant woman. For that matter, guards didn't seem to know the difference between a receptionist and a scientist. Put a lab coat on anyone and they look smart all of a sudden.

Jerome spoke up. "What's going on out there?" The guard ignored him.

Lisa walked up to Daniel, pulling a needle out of her pocket and popping the cap off. Daniel felt all warm and fuzzy inside. Well, maybe not warm exactly, but definitely happy. THIS was how a plan should go down.

She stood blocking the guard's view while she unlocked his wrist - sticking a key in his freed hand - and then did a terrible job of drawing his blood. Daniel could handle a little pain though.

Lisa turned, holding up the needle awkwardly to show the guard. If the guard had half a brain he'd know that wasn't standard procedure. Most of the building security guards were just high paid bodies, not PhDs. Daniel watched as Lisa approached Carl. She took another needle out, leaned into Carl, and then played her part perfectly.

Once Carl's wrist was free, he grabbed Lisa by the throat and pulled her on top of him, choking her. Daniel hadn't warned her about this part, making it so much more realistic when she started to scream.

The guard took a second to react. He hadn't expected trouble. He ran over to Lisa to try to free her. While the guard was pre-occupied, fighting Carl's grasp, Daniel freed himself from the rest of the restraints and crossed the room.

Daniel hadn't intended to kill him. He hadn't realized how hungry he was, and he was done eating before he knew it. The guard's death was regrettable, but made no difference in the long run. Lisa continued to scream, pulling with all her might away from Carl, who still had hold of her. She looked frantically from Carl, to the dead guard, to Daniel. When her eyes met Daniel's, he smiled with what he hoped was something reassuring. She stopped screaming, but then began hyperventilating. His blood mustache didn't help.

With her mostly quiet, he turned to Carl. "You can let her go now." Carl opened his fist, letting Lisa pull away to find the farthest wall to back up to. Daniel had to admit, he had thought the "character" idea stupid, and it still probably was. Carl, however, had made a convincing imbecile.

"And she's off limits." Daniel chastened Carl.

"Oh man!" Carl whined while freeing himself fully. "You know I'm starving and you took all the food for yourself." Maybe it wasn't all an act.

"We still need her." As soon as the words were out of his mouth, Daniel realized he'd made a mistake. Too late though.

Lisa started sobbing and talking all at the same time and the ruckus was giving him a headache. "Still?" Choke. Sob. "You said you'd let me go. You said I'd be safe."

After licking his lips clean, Daniel walked over to Lisa and put his hands on her shoulders in what seemed like a human gesture of comfort. She'd be of no use if she remained terrified, and he needed her calm.

"My dear, I was just trying to explain to my idiot friend why he shouldn't touch you. Of course you'll be free to go at the end of this."

Lisa asked, "And my husband?"

"So far you have done everything perfectly. We need to move now. We can discuss your husband when this is over."

As Daniel spoke, he directed Lisa to the door. Then he bent down to the dead guard, taking his badge and his gun. The badge would open most doors in the building – all the doors that didn't require a code as well. The gun, well, it would be nice to not have to get close to everyone he was going to have to kill tonight.

Daniel and Carl lined up behind Lisa at the door. Jerome, finally seeming to take in all that had happened, shouted out. "Hey, you can't just leave us here with that next door."

That had been the plan. Daniel hadn't thought to change it, but he had a point. Whatever was in the room next door was *wrong*.

Stephen interrupted his thoughts. "How long you gonna think about it?"

There was no time to think. So far, the guards hadn't noticed anything amiss, other than the distraction from the other room. Daniel moved fast. He freed Jerome first, and then Stephen. He didn't wait to see if they'd follow as he stepped out into the hall.

Chapter 8

Cate shook all over. She was on the floor, holding Andrew in her arms. Every inch of her vibrated with fear and tension. She didn't remember sitting down or cradling Andrew. He had a hole in his shoulder, near his neck, and blood was spreading across his shirt like an oil leak.

Cate knew, somewhere in her brain, that she should be doing something - trying to get bandages, calling for help, something. She just kept staring at the door, though, imagining what was beyond it, and remembering the last time she'd seen a man bitten.

He was only 18. Not really a man yet. She saw him so often, when she closed her eyes. Sometimes, it was happy memories: Mark laughing; asleep on the couch, where she so often found him in the mornings; or running, after a ball or away from a tag. Right now, the image that she couldn't shake was of the last moment she saw him – how terrified he looked. How his look pleaded with her to save him. How powerless she'd felt as the life drained from him.

Cate pushed the thought of her brother's death from her mind and forced herself to stop staring at the door. She needed to act, if only to keep from going insane. It felt like a million hours had passed, but it couldn't have been more than a few seconds.

Andrew was conscious but seemed to be putting all his energy into trying not to cry. He was taking long, gasping breaths. One guard was speaking into his walkie, while the other was just standing there, looking dumb. Another guard ran up from around the corner, and then stopped as he neared the group.

"Ma'am."

One of them was talking to her. It was the one she'd smiled at, the one who had opened the door for her just a few minutes before. Cate struggled to force her mind to hear him.

He said, "We're calling for an ambulance."

James and Stan both arrived, seconds later, with supplies, and she realized that they must've seen what happened from the observation deck.

Stan put his hand on her shoulder. "Let James handle this."

It was hard for her to process what he was saying. Slowly, his words sunk in and she understood that she needed to extricate herself from Andrew's body so James could help him. She pulled herself out from under Andrew and got him laid flat on the ground as James moved in beside him.

She hadn't stopped yet to think about anything that had happened. James was helping Andrew. Stan was looking at her, a million questions on his lips. The three guards stood conferring.

There was one phrase that kept repeating itself over and over in her head and it was all she could think to say.

"There's something wrong with the patients."

James, who'd already made progress cutting Andrew's shirt away from the wound, continued to work while adding, helpfully, "Ya think?"

The guard closest to her said, "The ambulance is on the way."

Stan said, "We don't know that." It took a second for her to understand that he was replying to her statement. "These are hardened criminals, death sentence criminals, maybe that guy missed getting out there and killing."

"But he didn't kill. He ate." As soon as she spoke out loud, she knew it was true. He hadn't bit Andrew as an act of violence or domination, he bit him for food. "He was feeding."

Stan was in full clamp down mode now. "We don't know that. And we are not discussing this here. Let's get Andrew out of the building and go back to the office to discuss this like calm human beings."

Cate wouldn't let him dismiss this. "We need a sample. We need to see what's in that blood!" Focusing on the work was the only way she could calm herself. She needed to study the situation, to understand the problem, and then, maybe, she would feel less horrified.

James finished taping up the bandage, stood up, and said, "She's right. I'll draw the sample."

Stan looked like he wanted to argue but instead he just said, "We're waiting for more guards before anyone goes back in that room."

Cate looked down at Andrew, essentially passed out on the floor. His wound was bleeding slowly, which was a good sign. If the prisoner had bitten into his carotid artery, Andrew would be dead. The wound needed to be cleaned and stitched, and Andrew needed antibiotics, far beyond anything they could do for him onsite. Still, she couldn't help but feel like letting him go to the hospital was a mistake. There was so much they didn't know, so much they needed to study, including now, apparently, Andrew.

And then another thought hit her. "We need to call Marisol." Stan and James exchanged glances. "I'm sure she's still here."

Stan jumped in. "I think we need to make sure that the situation is stable before going to deal with the bureaucrats."

Cate suddenly suspected Stan of covering something. The way he'd been acting all day, his response, or non-responsiveness, now, and his body language, all read guilty. Of what, she wasn't sure.

Before she could respond, Andrew started yelling.

"Hey! Hey. Heyyyyyy!" Cate could hear the panic and fear drowning out reason, but yelling "hey" was also uniquely Andrew.

Cate crouched down over him. "Hey."

He stopped yelling and looked at her. "Hey." Calmer, but still scared.

"How you doing? You all right?" she asked.

"I don't know. Am I?"

"Oh yeah. You're gonna be fine." She could see the relief in his face. "As my momma used to say, you'll live."

Stan crouched down beside her. "You know what happened?"

"Not really. Well, some of it." Cate saw Andrew's whole body tense up as he started to remember. "Oh God."

She shot Stan a dirty look before turning back to Andrew, speaking slowly and calmly. "Okay, okay. Don't think about it. We are going to get you out of here. An ambulance is on the way."

Andrew said, "It's after dark."

Not yet, but soon. The thirty minute alarm had sounded. Thirty minutes to leave the building if you were going home.

"We've still got time." Cate said, soothingly. "You're getting out of here while the rest of us will be stuck inside all night."

Cate smiled reassuringly at Andrew, but the end of day alarm complicated everything. The halls would be crowded with people leaving the building, making it harder for them to get through. The roads would be packed with cars from everyone heading home, making it difficult for the ambulance to get there. Andrew would be lucky to get into the ambulance before the sun set. There were thirty minutes until the doors were locked in the building, and everyone left inside would essentially be trapped there.

Stan was of no use. He was generally better at giving orders and talking on the phone, and right now she could see him defaulting to manager mode. Cate was glad James had volunteered to take the samples. She didn't feel ready to face what was on the other side of the door just yet. That left her or the guards, who seemed to think this emergency called for more whispering among themselves than anything else.

"I'll get a gurney." She stood up to go.

Andrew protested. "I can walk."

She, Stan, and James all said "no" at the same time. The synchronicity was enough to break the tension. They all started laughing. The laughing fit only lasted a second, but, for that second, she felt human again.

She headed to the spare lab room to bring a hospital bed for Andrew. Only after she rounded the corner, and could no longer hear the others, did she realize she was scared to be alone. There was no valid reason to be afraid at this moment. The doors were locked. She was safe. But she knew, beyond a doubt, that there was something wrong with the prisoners, the vaccinated prisoners, and she knew that what had happened to Andrew, and what had happened in that room, was at least partly her fault.

She found an unused hospital bed, and rolled it back towards Andrew, towards living, breathing people, as quickly as possible.

The first thing she noticed as she rounded the corner was that Andrew was standing up. He was bare-chested, except for the bandages, and so stood out among the rest of the men. The next thing she noticed was that there were several more people crowding the hall than when she'd left a moment ago, a female guard and two men in suits. Recognition stopped her in her tracks.

Mason was there, talking to the guards and Stan and James. She'd assumed he'd left. She was already shaky and didn't feel up to their first meeting in five years. She couldn't just stand in the middle of the hall like an idiot either. Eventually, someone would wonder what she was doing.

She pushed the bed closer. Andrew noticed her first.

"Thanks Cate." He slowly walked over and sat on the bed.

As she was getting Andrew situated, Mason turned his head, casting her a sideways glance, then turned back to his men as if she was of no importance. She was being silly, she knew, considering the craziness around her, but she was almost disappointed he hadn't reacted the way she'd always feared he would. He hadn't reacted at all.

"All right." Cate said. "Let's get you downstairs."

She started to walk away, pushing Andrew in the direction of the elevators, and then she heard her name. She stopped. She couldn't quite make herself turn around.

"Cate?"

And then Mason Farino was in front of her. The first man she'd ever loved, and the last. Walking away from him had been the hardest thing she'd ever done, and now he was here.

"Mason. Funny seeing you here. Sorry. I don't know what to say. Hi." She was an idiot.

"I never expected to see you at the NVIA." It was hard to read the way he looked at her. Disappointed, maybe? Or dismissive? "Last place I thought I'd ever see you."

"Yeah, well, it's been a long time." She almost snapped at him. She was too defensive.

"Yeah. I'm well aware of that." He smiled, as if to take the sting out. "I want to talk to you when you get back."

"You do?" Cate asked.

"I need to ask you some questions for my report." Of course! All those years of college and she'd forgotten how to talk to grown-ups. He'd be looking into the attack.

Mason looked at Andrew. "We'll catch up with you later. Don't want to slow you down at this hour."

He smiled, blankly. For an awkward moment, Cate stood there, not knowing if she was dismissed. She was saved from having to figure out the etiquette of this situation when a guard ran up to Mason. He whispered in Mason's ear, but Cate could hear him loud and clear.

"The vee prisoners are not in the lab." Cate was forgotten. Mason turned his back and walked away.

Andrew hadn't heard. Mason was conferring, furiously, with his gang of agents. Stan essentially scratching his head in the middle of the crowd. James was getting ready to go back into the room with three guards, guns drawn.

Cate took hold of the bed. "You ready?"

Andrew nodded, "Yeah. Let's get out of here."

Cate pushed Andrew towards the elevators. The bell rang. Fifteen minutes left.

Chapter 9

Daniel and Carl followed Lisa as she led them around a corner, down a hallway, past the reception area they had passed on the way in, and across the elevator lobby.

There were a half dozen people waiting for the elevator and they passed a few more as they continued on to the labs on the other side of the floor. No one noticed them. Everyone was focused on getting home to safety.

Daniel had been counting on the end of day rush to help mask their escape. The one possible wrinkle – well, one that Daniel had thought most possible - would've come if the researchers working with them had noticed them missing too quickly, but whatever had just happened in the room next to their prison lab had provided a bigger distraction than the one he'd worked out in advance. So far, everything was going better than imagined.

"You making a beeline for the exit or what?" Jerome prodded.

Well, not everything was going better. Why hadn't they gotten on line for the elevators?

"You don't need to worry about where I'm going. The exits are clearly marked, so feel free to head for one." Daniel not so subtly hinted.

"Nuh uh. I go out there now, I'll be caught in an hour." Jerome said. "I'm sticking with you. Seems like you might have a better plan."

Daniel fixed him with a discouraging stare. "My advice is to leave while you still can. Things are going to get very complicated very soon and you'll be better off on your own."

As the hallway emptied, the last of the lab workers on this floor vacated, Lisa badged them in to a traditional looking laboratory, with Bunsen burners and sinks and large refrigerators. She'd been instructed to find one that was on the same floor but not in use past sundown. As they filed into the room, Daniel considered locking Stephen and Jerome out in the hall. Jerome might cause a commotion, trying to stay by Daniel's side for some misguided reason, and right now Daniel needed to not be noticed more than he needed to get rid of a couple of annoyances.

Lisa opened a storage cabinet and pulled out a bag, handing it to Daniel. He hadn't been sure if they were going to be forced to wear prison garb, so Lisa had been told to bring clothes. Even though they didn't need them, Daniel was grateful for the change. He offered Carl his clean outfit, but Carl shook his head.

Daniel insisted, "At least change your hoodie. A different color might help you be less conspicuous when they do start looking for us."

Carl begrudgingly took the offered pile of clothes.

"You know, I can't get you into the room." Lisa said. She still smelled scared, but she was finally behaving like a grown up. "I can only show you to the door."

"Let me take care of that." Daniel replied.

He did have a plan for getting into the last room anyone would think he'd be headed for, but the plan would only work if everyone was as stupid as he always assumed they were.

"What room are you trying to get into?" Stephen asked.

Daniel didn't have time to come up with a perfect answer – one that would get Jerome and Stephen to walk away. He thought about lying, but it didn't seem worth the effort.

"Security Central Control."

Jerome looked at him like he was crazy, but Stephen just laughed. It wasn't a good laugh, like a "you're crazy, I'm outta here" laugh. In fact, it seemed to Daniel like Stephen just got a whole lot more interested in sticking around.

Daniel handed the bag to Carl and started to change his clothes while Carl pulled out lab equipment and started setting up. Lisa stayed close to Daniel, apparently trusting him more than the others, despite the fact that he was half naked.

Stephen turned to Carl. "And what's your part in all this?"

Carl smiled, like he'd been waiting for someone to ask him, and said, "I'm the brains!"

"Enough." Best to shut Carl up before he said too much. "Let's get this done."

Daniel mixed together the ingredients he'd had Lisa bring – mostly household items like sugar and fertilizer – and poured them into a large beaker Carl had pulled out. It only took a couple minutes before everything was set.

Daniel asked Lisa, "You know exactly how to get there from here? I don't want to take any wrong turns." Lisa was much easier to talk to now that she was mostly calm. She didn't start to cry or whimper or anything.

"I know where the room is. I walked there yesterday to be sure." She looked at Stephen and Jerome, and then back to Daniel. "Kind of conspicuous, the four of you together, don't you think?"

Daniel hadn't thought she had it in her. He was almost proud of her.

"Quite right. Gentlemen, this is where we part ways. I can't say our time together has been fun."

Stephen stepped in front of the door. "I think I'll go along with you. Could be interesting."

Daniel thought about killing him, but time was of the essence. "Fine. Jerome, it's been..."

"I'm coming too. I don't want to be left out."

Daniel couldn't help but get angry at their stupidity. "You will both be safer, faster, if you leave now."

"Really. It's gonna get scary in here." Carl said, and then smiled like he was being helpful.

Daniel could see the other two weren't budging, and he was out of time.

"If I can't get rid of you then I will ask that you remain as inconspicuous as possible. If at any point someone stops you, you're on your own."

"If you like that plan." Stephen wore a slight smirk. If Daniel didn't know better, he might've thought Stephen was the one who had all the answers.

"You think they know we're gone by now?" Carl was looking impatient.

Daniel answered. "Probably, but there are a lot of floors, and a lot of cameras to sort through, and we're not headed where they think we'd be headed. Let's get going."

Daniel opened the door and let Lisa take the lead. Jerome and Stephen followed. Once they were all out of the room, Carl set the beaker atop a lit Bunsen burner and followed Daniel into the hall.

As they made their way down the well-lit, beige colored hallway, Daniel was sure there were still a few day shift stragglers in the building, but he saw no one. That didn't mean no one saw him. He was aware of every camera, around every corner. There was nothing he could do about that – yet. Still, at times like this, the fact that vees looked human really came in handy. Even if they were scanning cameras for the missing vees, they'd have to confirm their identity. There was nothing, visibly, to distinguish them from any other humans in the building. And having a pregnant woman with them was a great coup.

They moved quickly, but didn't run. If they did happen to pass anyone, Daniel didn't want to draw any attention. In his estimation, they had about six minutes to make it to the room. They took the stairs down towards the basement level. There was no way to duck the cameras in the elevators and Daniel knew that security could command the elevators from Central Control, so the stairs were safer.

They made it to the basement without passing anyone. They had to be event more careful now. The maintenance and security personnel were centered here, and both groups tended to be well staffed at night. The basement, at least this part of it, looked almost exactly like the rest of the building, except that the beige walls were concrete.

LED lights inset along the ceiling made everything the same tone of blah. Really, whoever designed the building was a sadist. Daniel almost felt bad for the employees. Not really.

Daniel had worked in an office like this, when he was still human. Initially, when he'd been changed, he avoided human life as much as possible, other than for feeding. Eventually, he found he missed the daily interactions – since there hadn't been a strong sense of vee community at the time - and he actually missed having a defined schedule.

Unlike what some people might think, vampires do not burst into flame in sunlight. They are nocturnal. Day is night and night is day for the vee biorhythm. Daniel had tried to find fulfilling night jobs, but white collar jobs were rarely ever nocturnal, even in the good old days when humans knew little of the vee population. Once the vee infestation was let out of the bag, and the world changed to accommodate the fear and terror felt by the humans and encouraged by the government, nocturnal jobs became even more rare, and applicants for night time work were checked more closely for purity of blood.

As his life as a vee settled into a steady pattern of finding meals at night and places to sleep during the day, Daniel got bored. Really, as he thought about it, it became more clear to him that if the humans had just given him gainful employment, they might not be dealing with his mastermind plan right now. Kind of like if Hitler had become a successful artist.

Of course, he didn't want to compare himself to Hitler. Daniel preferred to think of himself as a decent vee. He wasn't trying to eradicate humans, just to get them to hear a few complaints they'd been ignoring for the last fifteen years or so. Sometimes a whisper was loud enough. He'd tried that already, and it hadn't worked. Tonight, Daniel was going to start shouting.

"We're here." Lisa stopped walking. "Or, it's right there. But, like I said, I can't open that door."

They were around the corner from his target. This is where his plan either worked or they went down fighting. The badge he'd taken off the dead guard was not enough to open the door to SCC. The lock also required a pass code that changed daily.

Daniel looked at Carl who looked ready to take on the world. Carl was from a different era – a much younger, brasher era – and didn't have a drop of sense. What he did have was brains, and a working understanding of modern security systems. There were few computer networks Carl couldn't turn into putty with his keyboard. But he didn't have sense enough to be nervous right now, unlike Daniel, who knew how important the next few seconds were.

He grew more nervous as time ticked by and they just stood there. The brightness of the lights made him feel exposed. Any second now, everything should change. He needed it all to change. If it didn't, there wasn't a plan B. Daniel turned to Jerome and Stephen, partly to give himself a diversion and partly to forestall any disasters.

"When we get in there, follow my lead. Just act like part of the team. You guys can be our bodyguards while Carl and I do all the work."

Stephen looked like he hadn't even heard what Daniel said, but Jerome said, "Works for me."

And then it was time. The smoke bomb had worked. Fire alarms sounded. Lights flashed. A firm, yet feminine voice of authority boomed, "This is an emergency. Please walk, do not run, to the nearest exit."

The door they were watching opened and armed guards, about fifteen by Daniel's count, started streaming out in one of three possible directions.

As a few guards began walking towards the stairwell that his little group was piled up in front of, Daniel started walking towards the open door just across the hall. He heard the rest of the group start to follow behind.

The guards walked briskly past, heading toward the stairwell. The last guard in line stopped, looking at Daniel and the rest of them. Since the situation was being "handled," the other guards continued on.

"Can I see your badges?" There didn't seem to be any more guards leaving through the open door. Only seconds remained for him to slip in.

Daniel didn't slow his pace. "Carl, show him, and then bring up the rear. The rest of you follow me."

Carl pushed the guard against the wall near the entrance to the stairwell. As the door to SCC was closing, the stream of guards temporarily staunched, Daniel managed to stop the door with his foot. He grabbed Lisa around the neck. She gasped, but didn't scream. That was okay. It wasn't time for that yet.

Carl fed on the guard, something that happened so quickly, he hadn't had time to make a sound. Daniel pushed Lisa through the open door, not letting go of her neck. Jerome and Stephen followed, with a bloodied Carl right behind them. There were a few men seated at computer screens, and a couple standing, getting geared up to head out. Overall, there looked like only half a dozen people in Security Central Control.

Daniel smiled at his audience. "Everyone stay where you are or I will rip this lovely woman's throat out while you watch."

The guards froze. Stephen smiled. Carl locked the door from the inside and Lisa screamed. His plan had worked out perfectly.

Chapter 10

It would take a long time to get to the exit. Everything in this building was far away from everything else.

Andrew was keeping quiet, despite the inquiring looks from all the people waiting for the elevator with them. Whatever thoughts he had running through his brain after the evening's events, he didn't want to talk about them. That was fine with Cate. She had a lot of thoughts of her own.

How could the vees have gotten out? Where were they now? How long had they been gone? Who let them out? That couldn't be what Stan was hiding, could it?

On top of that, there were the prisoners and the vaccine to consider. They'd missed something in their research. Or the new batch of vaccines had been contaminated. Or the prisoners all had something in their system that affected the vaccine. She needed to find out what had changed them into rabid animals that hadn't done the same thing to the pigs.

And then, of course, there was Mason. The last time she'd seen him had started as the best day of her life and ended as the worst. Everyone parted for them when the elevator got to their floor. As Cate pushed Andrew's gurney onto the elevator, memories of that last morning came flooding back to her.

Mason had taken her to the airport. She was flying home for winter break. He was driving to his folks after dropping her off. It wasn't a big goodbye. He was going to fly out to see her for New Year's, so it would only be a short separation.

As the last time she'd seen him, she often replayed every moment of that morning in her mind. He took her bag out of the trunk for her, hugged her tight, kissed her eyelids, and told her he loved her. It was like so many other moments in their year and a half relationship - perfect. She'd kissed him goodbye and walked away from him for what would be the last time.

If she'd known what was waiting for her at home, if she'd known how her life was about to change, she never would've left him. She would've held him there, in that moment forever.

When she wasn't careful, she ended up dwelling in that last moment, wishing he had grabbed her and said "Don't go," and, because this was a fantasy, she'd said "okay" and they'd spent that Christmas together. And, on New Year's Eve, he would've proposed, like she knew he'd been planning. She'd seen the receipt for the ring in his backpack. The memory of what could have been always led her to think of what had happened instead, and she couldn't bear to open that wound right now.

Cate and Andrew seemed to reach the lobby in record time, or maybe it was just that she lost track of present time while sifting through the past. There were three security guards at the front desk. They appeared to be waiting for Cate and Andrew.

One of the guards called out as they got closer, "The ambulance is at the gate."

Thank God. The ambulance had also arrived faster than Cate had thought it would, but she guessed cars got out of the way of ambulances - like people got out of the way of gurneys - even during rush hour.

The guard continued, "We'll escort you outside the building."

Cate squinted at him, confused as to why they'd do that. "Almost dark," he explained. "Don't want you getting stuck."

One guard stayed behind, glued to the bay of monitors – or perhaps to his chair - while the other two advanced before her. There were two sets of exit and entrance doors so one set was always locked. If someone managed to get past the first barrier without authorization, they'd be stuck between bullet proof glass doors.

They stood out front waiting for a few minutes while everyone lucky enough to be leaving headed towards the parking garage. When the ambulance finally pulled up, the EMTs didn't step out of the vehicle until one of the guards had walked the entire perimeter and declared it safe. Then the two EMTs hopped out and got Andrew lifted into the back of the ambulance.

Since he'd been so quiet, and she'd been lost in her thoughts, Cate hadn't noticed - Andrew was looking worse. His body was clenched like he was in pain, and he was covered in sweat like he had a fever. Furthermore, the wound was starting to smell. She guessed it was blood poisoning, in which case he'd probably be fine once he got to the hospital. Still, she felt guilty for not having realized how sick he was getting.

After the driver EMT hopped out of the back of the ambulance, Cate stepped quickly in and took Andrew's hand. "You'll be all right. I'll come visit you in the morning."

He didn't look reassured. He looked scared and in pain, so Cate did something totally unlike her. She leaned over and kissed Andrew on the forehead.

"Thanks. I feel better already." He managed to smile and Cate smiled back.

She squeezed Andrew's hand and started to step away. Andrew held her hand, keeping her in place.

"There's more wrong than you know." He whispered.

"What do you mean? Are you okay?" Cate asked, unable to come up with a better question, even though she somehow knew he wasn't talking about himself.

Andrew shook his head. "Be careful."

He closed his eyes and looked so sick Cate was afraid for a moment he would die right there. Cate turned to the EMT beside her, but he seemed unconcerned. Cate tried to come up with something more to say, or to ask, but her mind was racing in a million directions.

"Ma'am," the guard standing at the back of the ambulance called, interrupting her useless thoughts. "Gotta get you inside."

Andrew opened his eyes again, looked at Cate, and mustered another weak smile. She forced herself to smile in return, placed Andrew's hand on the mattress, as if putting away a fragile object, and left with the guards.

Cate wasn't sure why she'd kissed him. It wasn't some unspoken love for him. Andrew was just a co-worker, a sometimes friend. It felt like the right thing to do, in the moment. Strange as that had been, Andrew's warning to her was stranger still. What did he know?

She walked into the lobby, pushing the empty gurney. As soon as she and the guards had entered the building, the final alarm sounded. The doors locked loudly behind her.

She stood at the doors to watch the ambulance drive off. Into the sunset, she thought wryly, as she turned away.

"Thanks," she waved to the guards. "Have a good night."

Cate started heading back down the long corridor towards the elevators in her wing. She'd only taken a few steps down the hall, however, when the fire alarms started blaring.

Chapter 11

There were four vees free in the building, and one of them was a known terrorist.

"What next?" Frank asked.

So many bad choices. Mason had to pick one, though. Might as well start with the obvious. "Let's get security footage from SCC."

Althea took out her walkie and called down to security central. SCC had access to footage of everything that happened in this building. How well the guards there actually monitored was up for debate. Fortunately the computers captured it all digitally, even if no human eyes saw.

"Want to head down there?" asked Frank, all impatience.

"Yeah." He started to move that way and then realized he was being sloppy. Bad day to miss anything more. "No. In a minute. I want to check out the room first, and talk to everyone here."

"Your girlfriend already left," Frank smirked.

"What?" How could he know that?

"The cute brunette you were ogling earlier." Frank explained. "You want to talk to anyone else?"

Of course, he didn't know. He was just being Frank. "Yeah, even the boys. I want to talk to all of them."

Not that there were many left. With Cate and the injured guy - Andrew, he thought - gone, there were just the two staffers still here. Interrogating them without them knowing they were being interrogated would be the hard part. Always with this place, you needed to cover your ass and be politically safe. Ranks at the research facility were undisclosed. You never knew what level you were dealing with and you never knew who, within the entire NVIA, was willing and able to pay you back for doing your job with a bad report that could lead to a demotion, or worse.

Mason figured he'd get staff interviews over with first, but it looked as if the scientists were organizing their own raiding party. Stan, the old bureaucratic looking one, was addressing the three guards and James, the young, Ken doll looking scientist. Mason couldn't wait to see what this was about.

"Running drills?" Mason tried to make it sound like a joke instead of an official query.

Stan looked at Mason like he'd forgotten there were even agents around, as if what he was doing was more important. Of course, if they weren't involved, Stan and James would have no way of knowing about the escaped vees, having been confined in this area since the incident, and the guards having been told to keep quiet.

"We need to get a blood sample and, with the prisoners acting out physically," Stan made it sound like they were bad children instead of hardened killers, "I asked these guards to escort James into the room so there are no more injuries."

Mason could think of no good reason to stop them. Questions could wait a few minutes, while footage was tracked down. Seeing, and possibly interviewing, the person who'd ripped a chunk out of a fully grown man using only his teeth might prove useful.

Mason and Frank, with Althea as escort, had been on their way back up here to interview Daniel when the prisoner attack had occurred. When they'd arrived, the attack was the fire they thought they had to put out first. Daniel Trevore had been placed on the back burner for all of two seconds before Mason found out that that had been a mistake. Now, Daniel was free in the building and someone, maybe several someones, had helped him escape.

The building was locked down. The vees weren't going anywhere, if they were still even in the building. He had a little time. He'd try to run this investigation right. For now, that meant not stepping on toes while trying to figure out if, or how, what was going on here was related to the vee escape.

Mason waited and watched. The first guard opened the door and the other two guards pushed through, weapons drawn.

Mason hadn't expected to see anything quite so bizarre. All six prisoners were standing, staring at the door. They looked like they wanted to charge, but that something had stunned them. They were almost unresponsive, except that their eyes seemed to follow the guard's gun, with just a hint of recognition.

The remaining two guards entered the room and wrestled the closest prisoner to the floor, the one Mason assumed had been the biter. He didn't put up a fight.

Mason had plenty of things to deal with, but the behavior of the prisoners was something else. It was as if they were awake, but in a state of shock. Whatever drug they'd been given was obviously impacting their brains. They seemed almost lobotomized, except for the way in which they watched everything, their eyes following the action.

He looked at Frank, to see if his partner thought this was weird. Frank just looked amused. "Guess we won't be interviewing these guys."

James seemed to have the good sense to be scared as he walked through the door. He knelt quickly and efficiently drew the prisoner's blood, retreating the moment his vial was full. The guards backed out, keeping their weapons drawn, and the standing prisoners continued to stare.

The prisoner on the floor, Mason noticed, just before the door closed, had started licking the hole the needle had left.

James walked past Mason and Mason let him, turning, instead, to Stan.

"Can I have a moment of your time?" Always paid to be polite.

Stan sighed. "This is not a good time. Can we talk tomorrow? There's a lot to do right now." He looked off, significantly, Mason thought, in the direction James had headed.

Frank stepped in. "This will just take a minute. And it's very important."

Stan seemed to wage a momentary battle in his brain before fixing the fakest smile Mason had ever seen to his face. "Yes, of course, what can I do?"

"What can you tell us about the vees you have in the lab here?"

Stan looked surprised by the question. An honest reaction. "You could tell me more about them than I could tell you. I filled out paperwork requesting vee subjects and, after a very long wait, they were delivered. That's about all I know."

Mason believed him. Or, at least, believed him ignorant of what was going on.

Apparently Frank did too. "All right. You can get back to work. We're gonna need to speak with your colleague as well."

Again, the internal struggle. "He's going to be working in the lab for a while. Better not to ask him to leave what he's doing right now as we are short handed and this is time sensitive." Also caught in the politics of playing nice, Stan seemed to consider whether his answer was sufficient or not. He added, "I can show you to him."

"We can find it. We'll come by in a bit." Mason thought it best to get on with searching the room, and they'd have a lot more information after they got down to SCC.

He and Frank followed Althea around the corner to the room where the vees had been held, where a guard had died. Mason hadn't known the guy, hadn't even worked with him before today. The NVIA had more security factions than any other facility that he knew of.

There were the soldiers, who often acted as guards or escorts, but were also used in military actions like crowd control or storming vee hives. There were the security guards, who, for all intents and purposes were just like your average mall cop, only they got to carry real guns and were responsible for some very high security buildings. And then there were the agents - some like him and Frank, many others with vastly different job descriptions.

Althea stopped at the door to the room and waited, as if not sure she wanted to proceed.

Mason gestured at her badge. "Would you mind?" Mason's badge, unlike those of SCC guards, didn't work for every door.

Althea visibly steeled herself, swiped her badge against the reader and opened the door. As she took her first step into the room, Althea inhaled sharply and Mason realized that she'd lost a friend, or, at the very least, a co-worker today.

Mason put his hand on her arm, stopping her. "I'm sorry for your loss."

Althea looked him dead in the eyes. "He shouldn't have gone in the room alone. He should've waited."

She winced, like it hurt her to say it, but she stepped fully into the room and waited for him and Frank to follow.

Once inside, Frank let the door close. Mason knew that meant they were locked in, like the prisoners had been. There were certain rooms in this building that required a badge for entry and exit, for obvious reasons.

The dead guard was lying on the floor, head resting against the base of one of the hospital beds. His neck had been ripped open but there was very little blood – typical of a vee attack.

Frank knelt down near the body and looked up at Mason, a look of self satisfaction on his face. "No badge."

It was true. "Well, that explains how they got out of the room. How did they get out of the restraints?"

Frank and he examined all the beds, and each one looked the same. Frank said, "Magic?"

"Yeah." Mason replied. "Magic in the form of an assistant."

Frank looked over at the two way mirror. "I'd love to see that footage."

Mason was about to agree when the fire alarm went off. The blaring white lights flashing, the loud buzzing alarm, and the female announcer intently repeating that you should go was certainly effective at motivating a person to want to leave the building.

Mason had already walked out into the hall, to see if any of the guards knew what was going on, before he realized what had just happened. He'd walked out into the hall. He hadn't been able to do that a minute ago. The doors had unlocked.

Chapter 12

The takeover of Security Central Control had taken about ten seconds. Daniel was frankly disappointed. He'd hoped for a fight. He'd wished someone would do something truly unexpected. It had been too simple. Once the guards saw the pregnant lady in the hands of the evil vampire, they'd all rolled over and played dead.

Lisa, having served her main purpose, was now huddled in a corner of the room as far away from everyone as she could get. Stephen stood over the guards. If there was one thing Stephen seemed to be good for, it was making everyone around him uncomfortable, and if being scared kept the guards in line, Daniel was happy to let him stand there gawking.

The first thing Daniel had done, after breaking in, was to have Jerome get all the weapons off the guards. Daniel had him make a neat little pile of guns near where he planned on stationing himself. Then, Jerome and Stephen had handcuffed the guards, all but one, to each other, and to a railing between the main staging area of the room and a small step up to the two offices in the back, which Daniel assumed were for the managers. Next, they had to lock the door, which was a little more complicated than it might seem, as the lock required reprogramming. Carl managed with barely a complaint.

Daniel led the one guard he had separated out over to a chair near one of the phones. He'd picked this particular guard for his looks. He was handsome and appeared to spend a long time each day making sure he looked as good as possible. Vanity was a great weakness.

Daniel handcuffed him to the chair and said, "We're going to be needing your help. When this phone rings, as it will start doing sometime soon, we're going to need you to convince people that everything is copacetic. Understood?"

Of course, he hadn't. "I'm not gonna help you. None of us will."

Daniel dug his nail into the side of the boy's nose and ripped off a nostril. The guard screamed, of course. Daniel would have expected nothing less.

As the guard sniveled, pathetically, unable to tend his own wounds, Daniel spoke soothingly. "The bleeding will stop soon. I can't help with the pain. I can make it a lot worse. You have another nostril. You have more nose, for that matter. And ears. Very pretty, soft ears. The list goes on and on. Now do you understand?"

The guard just barely nodded, but it was enough.

There were about 30 monitors and computer screens in the room, all multitasking with security footage and architectural layouts of the building. Each computer could control everything in this building, if the operator knew how, and Carl knew exactly how.

Carl sat down at one of the consoles. Jerome took up a position next to Daniel, watching over Carl's shoulder. Not only was Carl, in Daniel's estimation, a computer genius, Carl was also an engineer and, thanks to a very complicated, long term plot involving drug addiction and blackmail, Carl was an engineer who had worked on installing systems exactly like this one in other secure office buildings.

Daniel was ready to start playing. "First thing's first. Lock the building doors so no one can get out."

The guards were all disarmed and handcuffed to each other around a metal railing that was cemented to the ground. Still, one of them tried to play hero. "You can't do that. People will die. There's a fire. You'll die too if you don't leave soon."

Daniel ignored him. He didn't care if the tied up guards figured out that there was no fire. The important thing was that all the people running for the exits couldn't know.

He said, "Show me the prison."

Carl brought up images of the cells. There were maybe 50 vees locked up. Most of them were pacing in the cells, or looking out through the bars. They heard the alarms, but couldn't go anywhere. There were only four guards in the prison at the moment, two on the far side of the door, and two in the cell arena. They all looked like they didn't know what they should do.

When the NVIA seized a vee, they could end up in this facility, in another NVIA building, or in one of several converted prisons around the country that had been updated to hold vees. Most vees who got arrested ended up in the more traditional style prison, if they were actually taken alive. It was supposedly illegal to kill vees who did not resist arrest, but most officers and agents ignored that rule, and most courts wouldn't punish those officers for their transgressions. Not that the prisons were much better than death. From Daniel's understanding, a traditional vee prison was like solitary confinement all day every day, only not as nice. Vees didn't tend to live very long in prison.

Through years of finding, bribing, and converting a small army of humans, Daniel had made sure he and Carl were brought here, to the NVIA research facility, where they performed all the testing. The humans needed lab rats, to find new ways to kill the vees, or fight them. They were all here to be poisoned, shot at, or dissected. Daniel had no idea of the body count, but the scientists who worked here could do whatever type of experiment they thought necessary in the name of finding a cure. Daniel had never heard of a vee actually being cured, of course. Nor had he ever heard of a vee leaving the research facility alive.

The world at large didn't know about the cells, and the experiments, or they pretended not to know. Today, Daniel would change that.

"Open the cells and the main door."

As Carl typed in the command, the guard with a hero complex started up again.

"You can't do that. Let the guards out first. They'll slaughter them."

He was right, but he didn't get to hear the witty response Daniel had on his lips. Stephen was at the guard's side in a second and before the breath from his last word had stopped moving, his throat was ripped and Stephen was draining him.

The other guards, tied together, started yelling, and kicking, and pulling at their handcuffs. When Stephen was done Daniel told Stepen, "Enough." An empty word, as Stephen was already moving away to sit down, but Daniel needed to appear in control, even if he was increasingly worried that Stephen was not controllable.

The guards were still restless so Daniel stood up and glared at them. They stopped yelling and kicking. They sat quietly watching Daniel carefully, as if waiting for the next slap from their master.

Daniel was pleased they recognized him as the leader. Still, he needed to keep absolute control. He turned to Jerome, who was standing near where Stephen sat, hungrily watching the victim's still warm body. Daniel said, "Jerome." Jerome turned to look at Daniel, who nodded towards the guards and added, "But don't kill him."

Jerome approached the bound guards and looked them over like trying to pick which of his harem wives to bring to bed tonight. The guards watched Jerome warily, each one trying to look as unappetizing as possible while keeping their eyes open to what was to come.

Jerome picked his victim, leaned over the young man, and whispered, "Don't worry, it will be fast."

The boy didn't have time to cry out before Jerome began to feed, but he screamed out the moment his neck was ripped open. The noise didn't last long. The boy was unconscious in under a minute. Daniel smiled to himself. He wasn't a monster, after all, and was glad Jerome didn't draw it out, didn't make it hurt.

There was a myth that being bitten by a vee was enjoyable, some would say sexual. Daniel assumed that lie came from vampire stories written long before the world knew the reality of vampirism.

Still, vees had followers. Young men and women who wanted to experience the pleasure of the bite. Of those who were allowed to live through the experience, Daniel assumed very few wanted to try it again. Being bitten by a vee was exactly like being bitten by a human who wanted to drink your blood. Your skin was torn and ripped and then your blood was sucked from your veins. Daniel had gone through it once himself. He wouldn't want to go through it again.

Jerome stopped while the guard was still breathing. And then he did something Daniel hadn't anticipated. He cut open his wrist and put the bleeding wound to the guard's mouth.

That was interesting. Perhaps he hadn't given Jerome enough credit. Daniel wished he'd thought of that himself. If nothing else, it should liven things up in here in the next few hours.

Daniel turned back to the monitors. He'd missed much of the fun. Two of the guards in the prison were dead already. The other two looked like they were favorites of the prisoners. Daniel didn't remember them in particular, but they were receiving a lot of special attention, and not enjoying it one bit.

"Why haven't they left yet?" he asked Carl.

Carl flipped through monitors and then found the answer. "The exit door was still sealed. Opening now."

As Daniel watched, the door at the end of the prison hallway swung open. No vees were in the corridor, but several looked towards the exit, as if hearing the movement of the door. The two surviving guards, if surviving could be used for their situation, were killed quickly and the vees started to file out.

Daniel watched the monitors for a moment as they cycled. A few humans here and there were moving quickly towards the exit and there were some guards roaming the halls. Most everyone seemed to be crowded in the lobby where the newly freed vees were heading, most likely drawn by the aroma.

The phone rang, interrupting the moment. Daniel turned to the guard in the chair and said, "You're on." Before he picked up the phone, before he gave the guard further instruction, he turned to Carl.

"Now, kill the power."

Chapter 13

Cate froze. She didn't smell or see a fire, and she was right near the door, so there was no need to rush. Still, the flashing lights and cacophony of alarms instantly set her heart to pounding.

She pushed the gurney against a wall and turned back towards the lobby. It had been an atypical day from the start. A fire alarm just after sunset, following everything else that had happened, was extraordinary.

The guards were in motion. One was directing and another was flipping through the monitors. The third was on his walkie. Cate approached their desk.

"Any idea what's going on?" she asked.

"Not yet, no," said the one that seemed to be in charge. "We're going to proceed with evacuating the building until we know more."

Cate assumed that the front doors unlocked automatically in case of an emergency, though she hadn't heard the click.

The guard in charge said, "You two head out and make sure all looks good. I imagine a lot more people will be down here soon." Turning to Cate, he added, "It'll be just a moment, ma'am."

Cate wasn't particularly worried about safety on the grounds outside, but the guards would want to be sure it was safe before sending everyone out into the night. The fire alarm triggering just after sunset felt like a trap to her, though she couldn't figure out how it would ever work. There was a perimeter fence, set up to deter any vees from getting on campus. There were guard towers manned 24/7. And so far as she knew, no vee had ever broken the perimeter. Still, there was a lot of open space out there, and she didn't like the idea of hundreds of humans standing outside at night with no solid walls to protect them.

The two guards reached the door and stopped. Cate heard one mutter to the other, "Locked." The second guard reached over and pushed on the door, but it didn't open.

They walked from one door to the next, trying each one in turn. All four sets of doors remained sealed tight. The guards, who probably knew more about the escaped vees than Cate did, must have guessed that there was something more going on here than locked doors, but to their credit, they didn't show it.

People started to arrive in the lobby. One woman. Two men. More were coming down the hall. The guard behind the desk said, "If you'll all wait here, we'll lead you safely out of the building in a minute."

The other two guards joined him and they conferred for a moment. One got on the phone again, while the other one went and positioned himself in front of the doors, as if to keep everyone away.

Within a few minutes, there were maybe twenty people standing around and a few minutes after that there were close to a hundred, by Cate's best estimate. On a normal day, Cate didn't like crowd's much. With everyone piling up in one spot, she found herself retreating towards the far wall.

There were too many people in one place and Cate felt trapped. As minutes passed and no progress was made with the doors, she backed up further, bumping into the gurney she'd left at the entrance to the hall. She pushed it a few feet in the direction of the elevators, to give herself space to move fast if she needed to. Some clawing instinct told her she might need to. She was still close enough to the exit to get out safely, if they got the doors unlocked and there really was a fire, but she felt better not being penned in.

The crowd started to sense that the guards didn't really know what was going on and the room hummed a nervous frequency. The casual conversations of co-workers, some of whom knew each other and many who did not, turned into agitated murmurings. Cate grew more uneasy. If they didn't open the doors soon, or make some sort of announcement, she was afraid there'd be a stampede. She backed down the hall a few feet further.

And then the lights went out. The crowd let out a collective gasp. There were red emergency lights that came on instantly, so the lobby wasn't pitch black, but the red glow leant the room a macabre feel.

A voice called out "What's going on?"

Another added, "Open the doors."

One of the guards at the front responded, "We're working on it," but his statement was muffled by the rising sound of frightened people. One voice speaking had turned into many shouting and fear changed the crowd in the lobby into a mob.

The mob started shouting, demanding to know what was going on, yelling that they wanted to be let out. The guards started yelling back, trying to calm everyone with their not so calm response to the situation.

Cate was terrified. She'd been trapped before, had seen family members corralled in darkness, and it felt like this. She started backing down the hall, keeping her hand on the wall for support and her eyes on the action so as not to be taken by surprise, which is why she didn't see the woman coming down the hall before knocking into her. Cate let out a short, panicked scream, before recovering her composure.

As Cate turned around, she realized she had backed into Director LaTrese, looking far calmer than Cate felt. "I'm sorry. I didn't see you." Cate felt almost silly for being panicked in Marisol's relaxed presence. "You startled me."

"What's going on in there?" Marisol gestured towards the shouting.

Cate turned to look back toward the main entrance, and that's when she saw it. There was a movement in the crowd, on the far side of the lobby, like a wave, or rather as if the mass of people at that end of the room had been hit with a battering ram. Even from this slight distance, she could see the pattern change.

A few people screamed in terror. Some yelled in confusion. Those on the far end of the lobby started pushing, frantically, towards the locked exit doors. The people in the middle, and by the entrance, not aware of what was going on, started pushing back and yelling. There was nowhere for them to go.

Cate could see what they couldn't. She knew why the crowd was pushing. She could see the vees pouring into the far end of the room. She saw the humans falling, as they were pulled into the tide. As one body got dragged down, the space was filled with a vee, grabbing at the next available blood source. The crowd was being overrun by vees who left dead bodies in their wake.

Cate grabbed Marisol and started pulling her down the hall. "Run." Why wouldn't she move? "Run. Vees!"

Marisol's face finally registered understanding and she turned with Cate and started running. They got to the end of the hall and Cate hit the elevator button. They could head to the stairs, but if the doors opened right away, she'd be safe inside a sealed box.

"There's no power." Marisol pointed out.

Of course. Stupid. She and Marisol took off running towards the stairwell. As they turned the corner, Cate stole a glance back toward the lobby. She heard gunshots, but couldn't see where they were coming from or if they were doing any good. As they rounded the corner, it looked as if the action were all contained in the lobby, as if no one had noticed them. She hoped she was right.

Chapter 14

If the door to the lab he'd just been standing in had opened without a badge, that meant that other rooms on this floor would be unlocked. Mason drew his gun and saw Frank, who was right behind him, do the same.

He didn't know what had happened to the drugged prisoners, but the idea of them roaming the halls scared him, not something he was used to feeling. Containing those prisoners became his first priority. Once that door was sealed, with them safely locked behind, he could figure out why there was a fire alarm going off in the middle of the night, on a night when so much had already gone so wrong.

Mason gestured for Althea, who was the only guard left in the hall, to fall in behind him. She looked like she was still in control, not freaked out by the noise and the flashing lights. That was good, because they were already wearing on his every nerve and it had only been seconds.

He inched along the wall to the corner. He was probably being overly cautious. There was no reason to suspect those prisoners had moved from the last time he saw them. They'd practically been comatose, but he didn't want to take any risks.

He peeked around the corner. In the academy, they'd taught him to take in a lot of information in a few seconds, to scan a room for potential danger. As he pulled his head back, he already knew there was nothing potential about this situation.

He turned to Frank, and Althea, and signaled them to be ready, and then he turned the corner. A second before, there had been one man lying on the ground, and a prisoner over him, tearing at his flesh. Now the prisoner was gone, and all that was left was the bloody remains of a guard.

The guard's body was right outside the prisoner's lab room. Mason had to assume the prisoner had retreated back into the room. There was no time for a human to have gotten out of sight anywhere else.

He moved forward slowly, keeping his gun trained on the door, but his eyes open in case anything moved down the hall or around the next corner. As he got closer to the body of the guard, it became obvious that there wasn't enough left of the man to even check for a pulse. His throat had been chewed off, almost down to his spine, and his shoulders and arms looked like they'd been blasted by a land mine. The prisoner hadn't bothered with trying to remove the bullet proof vest. He'd just eaten what was easiest.

The fact that the prisoner had eaten so much of this man so quickly was a thought Mason would have to process later, once he was out of danger. The door to the prisoner's lab room was closed and Mason waited until Frank and Althea were right behind him before pushing it open.

He moved into the room quickly. There was no one behind the door and the rest of the room, being fairly open, was easy to see. There was one prisoner in the room. He was standing on the far side, looking exactly as he had looked when Mason had seen him the first time, which must have been ten, fifteen minutes ago. He hadn't moved. He wasn't the prisoner Mason had seen in the hall.

Mason filled with doubt. Fear, really. Did he miss something when looking around the room? The other prisoner had to be here. He dropped down low and looked beneath all the hospital beds, but there was no one else in the room.

Mason turned to Althea. She should know more about the mechanics of the building. "How can we lock this door?"

For a second, she seemed thrown and Mason started running through all the crazy ideas he could come up with, like tying a belt around the handle.

Althea said, "I can do it. From the hall. We done in here?"

Mason looked around. The other five prisoners were gone, somewhere in the building. This one looked like he wasn't capable of moving, let alone killing, at the moment. Knowing what at least one of the others had done, Mason was sure it was best to lock him - and the others, when they found them - down as soon as possible.

Mason nodded. "Yeah, let's clear out."

The hall was still clear as they moved into it. Althea pulled the door closed and then entered a code on the keypad. The door locked.

Althea explained. "These are mechanical, so the fire alarm doesn't affect it."

Mason knew that not all doors in the building had a key pad – just the ones that needed to stay locked. Usually the keypad was disengaged, and only badges were used, but for special cases, and for people who knew how, they could be used for adding extra locks.

Frank was already edging down the hall, in the direction the prisoners must have gone, the direction the scientists had headed earlier. There were at least two other guards who should have been on this floor, and Mason had to assume they would also be found somewhere down that hallway.

Mason turned to Althea, "Mason." He nodded towards his partner. "You already met Frank."

She smiled. "Still just Althea."

They moved down the corridor together. Mason was relieved to have the extra gun.

Frank stopped at the first door they came to, waiting for Althea and Mason to back him up. As Frank opened the door, Mason's heart started pounding unexpectedly. In a way, this was a routine sweep. He'd hunted vees before in exactly this same manner. The situation was often scary, but Mason rarely was affected by nerves. He was too focused.

Seeing the way that guard had been ripped apart, seeing that prisoner tearing at him like a crow on road kill, had disturbed him in a way he thought he couldn't be disturbed anymore. He dealt with hunting vampires, creatures who drank human blood. He hadn't thought there was anything left that could freak him out. Mason didn't want to face that prisoner, or the four others out there.

Frank entered the room first, Mason close behind. Althea stayed by the door to make sure no one snuck up on them. The room was empty of life. It was a long hallway like room that had windows all along one side, overlooking the quarters where the vees had been held and where the one prisoner currently stood.

There was a door on the far side of this room, and Mason kept his eye on it as he scanned the rest of the room.

There seemed to be monitors and computers set up in the middle of the windows. Frank started fiddling with the keyboard, so Mason crossed over to the door on the far side, to make sure the room stayed clear.

Mason pressed his back to the door. He would sweep the hall in a bit, just not while Frank was distracted. His partner seemed pretty happy about something. "Check this out."

Frank pressed a key on the computer keyboard and one of the monitors shifted, or rather, the image displayed shifted to show the room with the prisoner in it. After some more fiddling, the prisoner started walking backwards.

Mason asked, "Can you bring up the other room?" The case could be solved a lot faster if they could just find out who had helped free the vees right here.

"I have no idea. Probably." Frank started pressing more keys, with no results.

Mason added, "Just don't break anything." Frank didn't have a great record with technology but, like everything else, he thought he was good with it. "We can always come back with someone who knows what they're doing."

Frank acted like he hadn't heard him and just kept hitting random keys until both monitors suddenly went black. "What the...?"

If it hadn't been for the lights going out at the same time, Mason would've been pissed. Instead, he just got a sinking feeling.

Almost immediately, the room and hall took on a red glow from the emergency lights, with periodic white bursts from the fire alarm. The good news was, the power going off seemed to shut up the ever present voice of the woman telling them to leave the building.

As Mason's eyes adjusted, Frank said "Well, I guess we're done in here."

Mason took out his walkie to check in with SCC. Maybe they'd know more about what was going on.

"Security. This is Agent Farino, come in."

He waited. Frank waited. There was silence.

"Security, come in."

Frank looked over to Althea, who had stopped watching the hall for a second to glance back at them. "Want to try yours?" he asked.

Althea took out her walkie. "Joe, Mike, you guys there?"

The walkie was silent. The whole floor was silent. Until it wasn't.

There was a loud crash, like shelves collapsing, coming from beyond the wall. Then there were several gun shots fired and lots of screaming.

There was no time to think, no time to try to figure out any of the mess that was going on. There was no time to be scared. Frank and Mason lined up behind Althea and they headed towards the noise.

Chapter 15

The guard on the phone performed his duty well. "Just a burner in one of the labs. Yeah, absent minded professor."

They'd promised the front door guards they'd send backup and unlock the jammed doors. Now they'd reassured HQ that there was no fire emergency. As far as anyone else was concerned, everything was still copacetic. Best to leave it like that as long as possible.

"Carl, can we kill the phones in the building?" Daniel asked.

"Yeah." He punched a few keys and presto change. "They should all be dead." Carl looked thoughtfully at the red phone on the wall in a box marked "emergency." "I can't do anything about that one – got its own power and connection. But aside from that, the only other working phone in the building should be at the fire command station."

Good. Carl had told him phones wouldn't be a problem, but Daniel hadn't remembered why. It would be unfortunate if the outside world found out what was going on before he was ready for them to know.

The power, of course, stayed on in the room. SCC had backup power. Lots of backup power. Even the monitors were still running, for a little while, allowing them all to enjoy the live show.

Daniel wasn't heartless. In fact, the best way to kill a vee was to take out the heart. He was feeling a little guilty being so pleased with all the slaughter. There was no other way to describe it, really. The humans in the lobby were pressed together like cattle. The vees were going from one to the next, taking a little bite here, sampling some blood there, treating the crowd like an all you can eat buffet. The humans couldn't even see it coming, but they were panicking like they smelled death. Daniel couldn't see details, with just the weird green camera light. Nonetheless, he enjoyed the entertainment.

Not all vees were vicious. In fact, most were reluctant blood suckers. Many had not wanted to become vees. Many tried not to kill. The vees Daniel had released had been imprisoned for weeks, months, as long as they were able to survive. They had been starved and tortured by the people working in this building. None of them would be feeling like a humanitarian right about now.

The guard, who was handcuffed near the phone, near the monitors, put his head down on the desk, closing his eyes tight. Jerome and Stephen moved around the monitors, and Stephen casually rested his hand on the guard's shoulder. The guard stiffened, but didn't move, which was probably best for him. Watching the massacre was like watching a great boxing match. The onscreen excitement made you want to get up and do something.

Stephen seemed to content himself with squeezing the guard's shoulder while he fixed his stare on the TV. Jerome actually walked away after a minute, as if he'd seen enough. Daniel didn't much care what either of them thought, but it was nice to have this moment witnessed by vees who might live to tell about it.

He realized that his methods could be construed as extreme. Better to make a statement than to continue being ignored. Fifteen years ago, when the vee "terror," as the humans called it, was sweeping Congress and the suburbs and even the Heartland, Daniel had tried speaking out as one sane voice to the masses. For a little while, he actually thought some kind of compromise could be reached, but he'd barely escaped with his head still on his shoulders and he certainly hadn't been heard by any sensible ears.

The humans, he'd come to find out, didn't want a compromise, a happy medium, a co-existence. They wanted a slaughter. And now, he smiled to himself, he was giving them one.

One of the tied up guards they were sharing the room with started to moan. Daniel didn't need to look to know why. He was the one Jerome had spared. He was changing, and the change hurt. Daniel ignored him, but the noise pulled his mind off the video monitors. Time to get to work.

"Carl." Carl looked up at him in response.

"Yup. I'm on it."

Carl started typing things into the computer. The computer screen went black and then a whole lot of code started scrolling across the screen while Carl typed and typed.

Daniel wasn't bad with computers. The whole internet had been a revelation for him and his nocturnal friends. He'd embraced that world as soon as the opportunity allowed. He was as susceptible to cute cat videos as the next person, but he mostly used the internet to gather information, read the pulse of the times, and to quietly – there were ways to be quiet online – spread his own messages, his own ideas. Yes, Daniel was quite good with some aspects of computing, just not the type of stuff Carl did. When Carl had tried to explain to him, several times, what exactly he planned on doing once they got into the SCC room, and how, Daniel's brain turned into a sieve.

The important thing was that Carl knew how to do what Daniel needed done. That's why Daniel liked him so much. He was useful.

"Hey, you okay?" One of the guards whispered to the moaner.

Now that Carl was writing in Greek, Daniel was easily distracted. He turned to see how the guards were handling the situation.

The one that was changing was collapsed forward, as much as he could be collapsed with his wrists handcuffed behind him. His immediate neighbor, the guard to his left, was trying to console him. Daniel found it laughable that the one considerate guard just wasn't looking ahead.

He said, "I'd worry more about yourself, if I were you." That got their attention.

One of them asked, "What do you mean?"

Jerome snickered and said, "Do you really not know?"

Four guard heads popped up all at once. It was like flashes going off, how fast the light bulbs over their heads appeared. One brave soul decided to address Daniel.

"You should take him with you. He's one of you now."

"What?" Daniel put on an expression of shock. "But he's your companion, your friend. You want to just turn him over to the evil monsters?"

The guard who spoke up looked away. He was done arguing, for now. The guard on the left, the one who'd been so concerned for his buddy just a few minutes ago, picked up the fight.

"If you're all about liberating the vees, you shouldn't leave him locked up here. They'll just kill him, or put him in prison when they take the building back."

Daniel walked over to the young man, who, to his credit, held Daniel's gaze. Daniel leaned in, close enough to smell the sweat building up on the man's neck, and whispered, "You mean, you'd kill him, if you took the building back. Only, you see, I am guessing that he's going to get hungry long before there's any chance of a rescue."

The guard didn't turn away, or break his glare, and Daniel couldn't help but admire him, for the briefest of moments, before he returned to Carl's side.

Lisa, who'd been hiding, as best she could in a room with no closets, walked slowly, and quietly towards him. He watched her approach, since the show on the monitors was starting to get boring. She looked as if every step pained her. He braced himself for what was sure to be a boring conversation about the value of human life or her baby or husband. Whatever she had to say, he didn't need to hear.

"Daniel." As soon as she spoke, all the vees except Carl turned to watch. It had been better for her when she was hiding.

"Daniel. Maybe you could let him go? You don't have to bring him along or anything. Just put him out in the hall?"

Daniel could hardly bear the weight of her naivety. "Have you ever seen a newly changed vee? They're like animals, starving animals. He'll eat the first human he sees. I let him go out there, he will kill. It might not be one of these handsome boys here, but he'll find something to eat. Maybe even you, if I have to keep answering stupid questions."

She started backing away, retreating to her corner again, when Stephen's hand reached out and grabbed her, hard, on her upper arm.

Daniel hadn't seen that coming either. These two were surprising him more and more, and it wasn't a good thing. Lisa gasped, but otherwise remained quiet as Stephen pulled her in close to his face.

"I could change you." Stephen practically licked his lips at the prospect. "Never seen what that would do to a pregnant lady."

"Let her go." Daniel felt like he had to take control, fast.

Stephen continued holding Lisa. He slowly turned to face Daniel, smile on his lips. "Why?"

Why not? Because I said so. Because she's mine. None of those seemed adequate. Stephen needed to understand that he was not the one in control. Carl had turned to watch the action. Jerome's eyes had been hooked from the start.

"You are free to leave whenever you want. But while you're in my house, you will not bother my guest." He hoped that didn't sound as weak on the outside as it was sounding in his head. He was letting this one get to him.

Stephen smiled a little deeper. He looked as if he was going to release Lisa and then he lunged into her instead. Stephen licked her neck. She yelled out, and started crying. Stephen let her go and she ran off to her corner.

Daniel considered killing Stephen. He couldn't trust him and he'd just feel better without Stephen around. Of course, if he killed him now, he might start to smell before they were done.

Carl went back to typing. Jerome went off to find a chair. Stephen stayed put, smiling at Daniel.

Daniel turned to Carl. "How much longer?"

"Hard to say. Ten minutes. Maybe twenty. I'll know when it's done."

Daniel let his hand rest on the pile of guns. Stephen was watching him, no emotion showing. Daniel, feeling caught, pulled his hand back and let it rest on the chair. He looked past Stephen, towards where Jerome was sitting. As if catching his cue, Jerome asked, "What are you doing with that stuff anyway?"

Daniel didn't care for Jerome one way or the other, but this might be a good time to make an impression, to gather a follower.

Daniel announced, with pride, "Carl is copying the entire NVIA database, and then deleting it."

Chapter 16

Cate and Marisol ran up the stairs. After a few flights, Marisol's breathing was getting loud and Cate was starting to feel like every vee in the building would hear her.

"Let's slow down." Cate gestured to Marisol's heels. They weren't especially high, but they were noisy and probably slowed her down. Cate was wearing tennis shoes, so wasn't worried about her rubber soles. Marisol took the cue, stopped and took her shoes off.

"There's an army of vees out there." Marisol expressed disbelief. "Someone must have opened the prison up."

Cate hadn't really thought about where the vees had come from, only that she needed to get out of there.

"Maybe the fire alarm opened the doors?" Cate suggested.

Marisol considered for a moment. "No. Not all doors open, certainly not in the prisons. We should..." Marisol looked up the stairs to finish her thought.

They started running up the stairs again, with much less noise now. Cate focused every ounce of energy she could spare into listening past the footsteps, listening for any noise that could suggest danger.

Physically, vees were like humans at their peak, if humans felt no pain and were flooded with adrenaline, so they could push beyond normal limits, running faster, lifting more weight, enduring longer without food or rest, and healing more quickly. It wouldn't be hard for a vee, or several, to catch them in this stairwell, even with the head start they had. Her only hope was that the vees were still too distracted in the lobby to go sniffing for fresh food.

As they reached the third floor landing, Cate's skin began to prickle. She gestured Marisol to stop. The two of them stood there for a second, holding their breath, and then Cate was sure of it. She had heard, or felt, a door open. Now she heard it close. Somewhere, someone had entered the stairwell.

They were in a trap. In the stairwell, they could only run up or down. Down was obviously bad. Up meant they stayed in a narrow space with no place to hide, or cover their sound and smell. Cate opened the third floor door and ushered Marisol out of the stairwell.

"What's going on?" Marisol had the good sense to whisper.

"I don't know," She couldn't be sure. "I heard someone on the stairs."

"I don't hear anything." Marisol whispered.

Cate said, "Trust me, there's someone coming."

Cate wasn't familiar with this floor. She usually went right to her office, sometimes to the cafeteria, rarely to the gym, and occasionally to a meeting somewhere in the building away from her lab, but she didn't usually have time to explore. This looked like a call center. It wasn't, of course, they didn't do things like that here, but the floor was miles of cubicles in every direction, so far as she could tell.

"Maybe we can hide? Maybe he didn't hear us?" Marisol sounded scared, even if her voice didn't shake.

"They can smell us." Cate wished she had something more reassuring to say. "Our best option is to get as much distance between us before he catches our scent."

They were already moving away from the stairwell, crossing the cubicle field. The building was set up like a giant "H" with stairwells at the intersection of the middle line with each of the two vertical lines. The next closest stairwell should be straight across the field of cubicles. That seemed like an option, at least.

"Maybe it was just another person, getting away from that mess in the lobby?" Cate said, for Marisol's benefit.

Marisol gave a little smile, like she knew what Cate was trying to do. Cate might've continued to speculate, if she hadn't just heard the door from the stairwell, the one they'd just come through, open and close again.

"He's here." Cate whispered.

Cate grabbed Marisol's arm and began running. If it were a vee, they couldn't outrun it, or hide. He would smell them out. They might have a chance of getting somewhere, finding someone, or figuring out something before they were caught.

They sprinted down the corridor, past the next stairwell, into another field of cubicles. They turned into one of the rows of cubicles, ducking down below eyeline, and started navigating the maze, hoping the maze would confuse the vee as much as it confused them. Once they were thoroughly enmeshed in the rows of desks and chairs, Marisol pulled away from Cate and stopped.

"We should separate," Marisol whispered.

"That's a terrible idea."

"Listen," Marisol hissed. "It can only track us one at a time. Separating might slow him down, give one of us a chance."

Cate was about to disagree more emphatically when she saw Marisol's face change. She looked horrified. And then Cate felt herself pushed to the ground, as if she had been used as a launch. Her face was still pressed into the floor as Marisol began to scream.

There was no one on top of her, after that initial push. Cate recovered from the shock of falling, stood up, and saw the vee. He was big, maybe 6' 2", and he was choking Marisol with one hand, forcing her to the ground. Marisol's knees gave out and, as she collapsed, the vee leaned over her.

Cate launched herself at the vee. She flew into the side of his bent over body, knocking him to the ground, landing on top of him. As she kept pressure on his chest, she looked around for something to hit him with.

"What are you doing?" He asked, as if he were sincerely confused.

The only thing Cate could find and grab was a computer keyboard. She ripped it out and raised it over her head, but the vee was no longer confused. He grabbed her by her shirt and threw her into the nearest cubicle.

The back of her head hit the desk, as her body pushed the rolling chair across the floor. Cate lay crumpled on the ground.

That's when the gun fired. Cate didn't see what happened, but when she turned towards the sound, Marisol was standing, holding a gun, and the vee was lying on the ground, blood pouring out of his chest.

"You had a gun?" It was the only thing Cate could think to say.

Marisol regarded her as something of an idiot. "Obviously."

Cate slowly moved closer to the vee, trying to see if he was, in fact, dead. She was looking at his body, thinking it would be pretty hard for him to have survived, so she didn't see Marisol move. When she stood and turned around, Marisol had backed up a few steps and was now holding the gun pointed at Cate.

"What are you doing?" Maybe Marisol was just confused, scared.

"Your whole department is just a giant headache." Marisol didn't waver. "First the pigs, and now this."

"I don't understand. The pigs? What are you talking about?" Cate asked.

"So you weren't in on Stan's little secret? I guess that doesn't really matter now."

Cate was frightened, more so than she'd been a few seconds ago, facing down a vee. Then, she hadn't had time to think. Then, it was all adrenaline. Now, she was facing a colleague who was calmly staring her down across the barrel of a gun.

Marisol had changed. There was no fear in her. She held the gun on Cate and was in complete control of the situation. And understanding that, Cate knew what had changed, and knew what was coming next.

"Now," Marisol demanded, "Why don't you explain to me how you tricked the NVIA into hiring a vee?"

Chapter 17

It wasn't the entire database, of course. That would probably take days to back up. They were stealing names and addresses of agents, as well as information on all suspected vees. That was one part of it. The other part was data associated with the research no one knew was going on here. That would all have to change.

The public hated when poor innocent monkeys were tortured for science. There were a lot worse things going on at the old NVIA, and no one would ever know about them if Daniel didn't help that information get out.

"So, you just copying files?" Jerome asked.

"Copying and deleting, yes. Wouldn't want them to be able to access that information again, would we?" At least, not to the files they only kept here.

Jerome thought for a minute and then asked, "Don't they have backups?"

Daniel smiled. "They do. We're going for those next."

The problem with buildings like this one is that they kept their own backups secure by keeping them on the premises. They couldn't be "hacked" from outside, at least so far as Daniel understood it. Of course, he wasn't on the outside.

Daniel glanced over at the monitors. The carnage in the lobby seemed to be wrapping up so Daniel said, "Unlock the front doors."

A few keystrokes later and Daniel saw a couple of the vees trying the doors. When they opened, most of the vees started to leave, though a few hung around, checking bodies for loot.

Stephen, apparently bored with Carl's typing and with the winding down of action in the lobby, started playing with the handcuffed guard's hair and neck, running his fingers over him. The guard started sniveling.

"Leave him alone."

Stephen glared at Daniel. "He's in my way."

Daniel ordered, "Then handcuff him to the rest of the guards."

Daniel was surprised that Stephen looked willing to comply. He unhooked the guard and walked him over to the cluster of chained up guards. The one Stephen was escorting started yelling.

"Hey. No way. I did my job. I did my job."

Daniel looked over to see what he was so upset about and realized Stephen was handcuffing him to the guard who was mid change. Ah. That would explain his willingness to cooperate. He was designing his own show. Still, the guard had done his job.

"Put him at the end." Daniel called to Stephen.

Stephen stopped, mid cuff, and without a word, moved the guard to the end. The guard, for his part, looked mollified, but also like he felt too guilty to face his fellow guards. None of them said anything to him, though. Perhaps they realized they would've done the same.

Stephen began pacing in front of the guards. Daniel wasn't sure why he cared one way or the other about what happened to Lisa, who was still hiding in her corner. Strangely though, he was relieved they weren't going to have to have another talk about her.

The guards, on the other hand, deserved a little torture. They knew better than to make eye contact with Stephen. In a way, it made Daniel sad that they weren't as scared of him, but even humans could smell the evil on Stephen.

Daniel knew Stephen wouldn't be hungry yet, so he wasn't planning on feeding. In fact, Stephen reminded Daniel of a cat who'd caught a mouse and wanted to play.

"Which one of you would like to die first?" Stephen asked, casually.

Daniel watched, dispassionately, as Stephen walked along the line of guards, evaluating each one. The guard who was changing looked like hell. That was typical. He didn't have long to suffer in pain. Soon, all he'd know was hunger.

Daniel remembered it like it was yesterday. The one concern he'd had about being changed was whether or not he could feed on a fellow human. It seemed like such a silly thought now, for so many reasons, but at the time, he thought killing would be difficult.

As soon as he woke - if that's the right word for feeling like you are dying for an endless number of hours and then, suddenly, feeling alive – as soon as he woke, the first need he had was to eat. He craved nothing more than to bite into a juicy neck or arm or leg. If a toddler had walked by, if a family member had been near, Daniel would've thought nothing of killing it, just to feed the hunger.

Fortunately, Kenneth had known he'd be hungry and had had two humans he'd considered expendable, humans who hadn't kept Kenneth's interest enough for him to care if they lived, ready for Daniel. Daniel hadn't had to hunt for anything that first night. He hadn't had to go looking for food when starving practically out of his mind. There had been many times since, when a food source was hard to find - times when he'd felt hunger again. Those nights came later. On his first night, he'd been well fed.

Stephen leaned over the guard to the right of the soon-to-be vee. The guard didn't look at him, so Stephen grabbed his chin and pulled until the guard had no choice, their faces close.

"Would you like me to save you?" Stephen asked. "I can move you."

Stephen smiled. The guard looked like he was going to cry. Stephen moved on without waiting for an answer, turning to the guard to the left of the soon-to-be vee.

"Or you? I could save you." Stephen stood up. "But not both of you. Just the one I like better. Can either of you give me a reason to like you?"

Daniel watched, fascinated. He didn't consider himself kind. Not even when he was human. He'd always been too selfish to be kind, but he wasn't cruel. Stephen was a good villain. He had no discernible sense of morality.

Neither guard spoke, though surely, the one on the right, who had started crying, wanted to. Stephen kicked the guard's foot and he started sniffling, but didn't look up and didn't speak.

"Not even a little begging?" Stephen walked over and kicked the other guard's foot. "You just have to grovel for a second or two and you'll be better off than the rest of these guys."

Daniel looked at Jerome, to see how he was enjoying Stephen's show. He was pleased to see a look of distaste hiding behind Jerome's passive expression. That was the word for what he sensed growing in himself, distaste. He didn't care if the guards all died, but at some point in his life he'd learned it's not polite to play with your food.

Still, he wasn't ready for another confrontation with Stephen. He needed the rest of this night to go smoothly. It had been a mistake taking the two vees with him. Now that he was stuck with an entourage, they needed to follow him. Too many things could go wrong if they cast out on their own, or worse, tried to take control. Jerome was a follower. That was obvious. Stephen, on the other hand, was playing his own game.

Instinctively, Daniel checked on Lisa, crouched in her corner, hands over her ears. Hear no evil, see no evil didn't mean you were safe from evil. If it kept her quiet, he wasn't about to point that out, especially because just then, the moaning started. It sounded like someone fighting to wake up from a nightmare. The guard was about to become a vee.

"Uh oh." Stephen stood over the guards. "Looks like time's up."

The guards to either side starting moving away, as far as their restraints would take them. The one who had been crying just a moment ago, caved.

"Let me out. Let me out." He was leaning as far away as possible and yelling at Stephen. "I'll do whatever. Please?"

Stephen just started laughing. Daniel noticed Carl had turned around to watch. Jerome was still transfixed. Stephen walked to the nearest desk and sat down to observe from a distance.

The new vee stopped moaning and lifted his head. He appeared, to Daniel, like he was strung out on some drug. His eyes were unfocused, his mouth agape. He didn't seem to know where he was.

Then he perked up, like an idea had just occurred to him, or he smelled a cup of fresh brewed coffee like all those happy humans on TV commercials. He turned, slowly, and looked at the guard to his left, who was practically lying in the lap of the guard beside him.

The vee lunged for him, not realizing his arms were secured behind him. He missed when he was stopped by the cuffs. He tried again, catching a tooth on the guard's sleeve, ripping his shirt. The human guard pulled away further, lifting his legs in an athletic feat Daniel was sure he could never accomplish, and kicked the vee in the face. It had the effect of temporarily stunning him, and the guard kicked him again.

The vee sat up and turned the other way, facing the crybaby, who instantly started pleading with the new vee. "Joe. C'mon man. You don't want to do this."

Joe was beyond hearing. He lunged at the guard, catching his shoulder and scratching it. The guard flailed out with his legs, kicking at Joe, managing only to kick him as high as his thighs, which had the unfortunate result of tipping Joe closer to him.

Joe lunged again, and this time he caught the guard's cheek, ripping it open. His face started to bleed, and the guard began screaming. The guard on the other side of Joe tried kicking him again, Daniel assumed to distract him, but now that he had tasted blood, nothing would turn his attention.

Joe managed to simultaneously prop his legs under him and lunge at the screaming guard, which gave him just enough leverage to bring his mouth down on the guard's neck. He sank his teeth in and began drinking.

The guard's screams eventually grew more quiet until, finally, they died. The only sound clearly heard was the sucking noise the new vee was making as he drank up what was left.

Stephen got up and walked over to Daniel. Like a spell had been broken, everyone seemed to come to life at the same time. The surviving guards started openly weeping, moaning, or staring away from their dead colleague. Carl turned back to the computers. Joe finished his meal and sat up, looking out at the room like he was starting to get his vision back.

Stephen smiled at Daniel and said, "You're welcome."

Daniel was still trying to figure out what he meant by that when Stephen turned, walked back over to the guards, and unlocked Joe, who looked dazed. Joe stood up, and fell over, and then stood up again. Stephen supported him, like a friend, holding him up. He ripped off part of Joe's sleeve and handed it back to him.

"You might want to wipe that off," he said, gesturing to the blood smeared all over Joe's face.

"Hmm?" He held the cloth in his hands, confused.

"Wipe your mouth, kid." Stephen said, not unkindly.

Joe responded without thinking, taking the cloth to his face and wiping. When he pulled the rag away and saw the blood, his eyes widened in terror. He turned around, starting to comprehend and, seeing the dead guard he started yelling.

"Oh my God. Oh my God. I didn't mean to. I didn't. I couldn't do that."

He made as if to check on the dead guard, as if to help him. Stephen turned Joe to face him and said, "It's all right, kid. You're on the right side now."

Joe didn't look convinced. He turned towards his old pals, as if gauging whether he could go back to them. Clearly, he couldn't. So he turned, again, to Stephen, who led him over to Jerome.

"New recruit." Stephen said, winking at Daniel.

Daniel watched as Stephen sat down next to Joe and Jerome and started - from the way it looked to Daniel - buttering them both up. After a few minutes, Stephen turned to Daniel, as if he knew he was being watched. Stephen smiled at him, all innocence.

Daniel smiled back. He knew Stephen was playing a game, though he didn't know what Stephen's rules were. No matter the game. No matter the rules. The trick, Daniel knew, was to make sure he was the one with the winning hand.

Chapter 18

Held at gunpoint, it becomes hard to find the right words, to build a defense. Cate's mind went blank. She came out with the only thing she could think to say. "What?"

Marisol was unimpressed. "You can see and hear things I can't. And no human moves like you just did, fighting that vee. Your neck should be broken."

"Marisol." It was a long shot, but she didn't have a better defense. "I was saving your life."

It looked like a smirk, so Cate wasn't sure if Marisol meant it to be reassuring or demeaning.

"Thank you for not letting that vee eat me. And you're welcome for my shooting him for you. Now we're even." Just a touch of sarcasm. "You want to answer some questions for me, or should I just walk you down to the prison right now?"

Cate had lived so long as though she were human, spent so many years working at her top secret job with high security clearance, she'd grown accustomed to being safe. The first year had been the hardest. After she'd faked her way in, she lived in constant fear of discovery. When she'd eventually realized how easy it was to go undetected, she'd let her guard down, and now she was caught.

Cate said, "Marisol, I...I think we have more important things to worry about right now."

Marisol looked around, taking in the dead vee next to Cate, as if wondering if there were any other vees in the room. Then she retrained her eyes on Cate.

"If you were the old Cate, the human Cate, I would agree. But you being a vee, there being vees on the loose because someone on the inside let them out, makes me think this is the most important thing right now."

Cate pleaded, "You have to know I had nothing to do with that. I would never..."

Marisol snapped, "What? Never help your fellow vees? How could I trust anything you say to me? You are one of them!"

Cate cried out, "Vees killed my whole family."

After Mark, and Mom and Dad had been killed, Cate had gone to stay at their neighbor, Sarah's house. The NVIA was a relatively new agency at the time. There weren't a lot of field offices, so an agent had teamed with a local detective on her case. They'd asked her a bunch of questions about the murders, and she'd told them what she could about the vee. She described him to them. They made a composite picture of him, that looked eerily like him. Ultimately, though, they didn't know who he was or have a record of him. They told her they were working on catching him but they hadn't left her with much hope.

"You are a vee." Marisol's words hurt, even though they were true.

"I didn't choose this." Cate insisted. "It was forced on me."

It was a few days after the murders when Cate returned to what had been her family home. She wouldn't have gone back so soon, but she needed clothes for the funeral, and money. Until the will was worked out and insurance dealt with, she was living on her last work study paycheck. Dad had always kept a few hundred dollars in his sock drawer, so Cate planned to grab that, along with a black dress.

It hadn't occurred to her that the vee would be there. It was daytime, and lightning doesn't strike twice in the same spot. He'd "enjoyed watching her," he said. He enjoyed watching her watch him kill her brother. She thought he hadn't noticed, but he had. "He knew what she needed," he said.

He bit her, and she was glad, happy she would be with her family. She wanted to die. Then he did something more horrible than killing her. He offered her his blood. Despite wanting to die, she drank it. She drank because she didn't have the courage to die. She drank because she knew it was her only chance to live. She would never think of that moment without being overwhelmed with guilt for having chosen to live. In that moment, when she was done drinking and realized that she would live, she felt like the most horrid person in the world, like there was nothing more horrible she could do than what she had just done. She turned out to be wrong.

"Marisol, I would rather die than kill a human." Again, she thought to herself. I will never kill a human, again.

The vee left her alone in her house. She didn't know exactly how long she'd lain there. It was getting dark by the time she dragged herself up. The world was changed. She was confused, dizzy, hungry. She needed to get to safety. She walked to Sarah's house. She only wanted comfort. She only wanted a friend. She hadn't meant to hurt her. She hadn't meant to kill.

Marisol was still listening to her, which was good, even if she didn't seem to understand how deeply Cate meant what she said.

"I would rather die than live as a vee." If only she had. She wished almost every day that she'd died along with her family. Sarah's death, of course, had been blamed on the same vee that had killed Cate's family. It was an easy lie to tell, and easy to believe the poor grieving girl who had seen so much death.

Cate continued, "That's why I came to work here. I'm not trying to help them. I want them all dead, and I'm willing to die along with them."

It wasn't a truth she normally let herself think about. Of course, that's what would happen if the vaccine succeeded. She would starve along with the rest of them.

Marisol stared hard, as if trying to decide whether or not to believe Cate. It seemed like long hours went by with neither of them moving, before Marisol broke the silence.

"How did you do it? How did you pass the blood tests?" Marisol asked.

Cate explained, "I only had to pass the one."

Marisol's face registered understanding. "You process the blood tests in your lab."

"Yeah, periodic testing hasn't really been a problem for me."

Marisol pushed, "But the first one? How did you do that? Did Stan help you?"

Cate answered, "Stan? No. I didn't even know him yet. I inserted a bag of human blood under my skin. I really didn't know if it would work. I guess it did."

"Well, we'll be changing the way those tests are run in the future." Marisol seemed to run out of steam as she sank into a nearby chair.

Cate was stuck. If she pushed Marisol too hard right now, she could end up dead. Like Cate herself, Marisol had probably not worked in the field as an agent, but it was obvious she still remembered how to fire her gun. All agents, even researchers like herself, had to learn how to handle a weapon. Working for the NVIA in any respect was dangerous. Living in this world of monsters – of human or vee variety - was dangerous too. Still, a trained human with a gun trumped a reluctant, unarmed vee in the weapons department. Cate would have no chance if she tried to run. And she wouldn't attack. It felt like there was no good course of action. Whatever they did was up to Marisol to decide.

"What now?" Cate asked.

"Hell if I know. Any other day you'd be in the jail already, or I'd have shot you. Lucky for you we have a few other issues that I'd rather not deal with alone."

Marisol looked around for a moment, as if gesturing at the danger in some vague way, while also trying to spot an attack. Cate tried to convince herself that Marisol hadn't meant everything she'd said or, at least, not the part about shooting her. Either way, standing around wasn't going to improve anybody's situation.

"I don't think we should stay here." Cate suggested. This long hall of cubicles felt too open for safety.

"Since we can't get out of the building, and since there doesn't seem to be a good option, I'd say we should go back to the lab." Marisol paused, as if trying to work out a difficult math problem in her head. She continued. "Maybe you can help figure out what happened to those prisoners, or at the very least, I can have a long talk with Stan, if he's even there."

Cate asked, "Should we try a new set of stairs or go back to the one we were in before?"

Marisol waved towards the far stairs, the untested stairwell. She kept the gun trained on Cate.

"If there are vees out there, you can sniff them out before me." Marisol commanded. "I'm not putting this away. I don't trust you, and I'm holding this for whoever else we run into."

"Fair enough." Cate started to walk towards the stairs, aware of Marisol following, eyes, if not gun, trained on her.

They would have to be quiet once in the stairwell, and wouldn't be able to talk. There was something Marisol had said that was still bothering her. Cate stopped and turned back to Marisol.

"What?" Marisol's breath caught. "Did you hear something?"

"No. Sorry. No. I just had a question." Cate explained. "Why Stan? You brought him up a few times."

"You really don't know? About the pigs?" Marisol asked.

"You mentioned them earlier too. And no, I have no idea."

Marisol answered, "He's another problem I'll have to deal with when this is over. He lied about the pigs. I didn't know who in your department knew. I assumed he had help from one or more of you."

"What do you mean?" Cate felt like she had a right to defend herself. Her work was always impeccable. "I was there. The vee died when he had the pig's blood."

Marisol shook her head. "No, Stan didn't lie about the vee. He lied about the pigs. About what happened after your test."

"I don't understand. We euthanized the pigs. They were sent to be incinerated."

Marisol practically snorted. "And as Stan found out, and I found out later, that didn't go so well."

"The incineration?" What could have possibly gone wrong at the incinerators? "Did the pigs explode or something?" Cate asked.

For a moment Cate thought it seemed as if Marisol was savoring the suspense, like an actor about to deliver the line of her life. And in truth, nothing Marisol could have said would have surprised Cate more.

"No, they attacked. The dead pigs got up and attacked the technicians."

Chapter 19

As they moved down the hall, the noises they'd been hearing disappeared. There was no more gunfire, no more crashing. Mason couldn't guess if that was a good thing or bad. He just knew the quiet made it harder to find whoever had been making the noise.

Althea stopped at the next door down. Frank moved past. Mason waited. This was all part of the drill now. One person takes point. One person watches the back. One would be the sweep. He had to hand it to Althea, she was much better than a glorified mall cop.

Althea opened the door. Frank stepped in. Mason waited until Althea was in before he moved to his post at the door.

Mason kept his eyes on the hall, but glanced into the room, periodically, to study everything, check on his team, and look for danger. Mason had always been good at spotting danger.

In the agency, they don't call you a rookie when you're new to the field, but they treat you that way. It's not that you automatically get assigned all the crappy, dead end leads. It's completely random. "Beginner's luck," it was ironically called. Yet everyone knows it will be months or even years before your luck will turn around.

Frank was Mason's first partner. He'd graduated the academy the year before Mason. Everybody liked Frank, but in the year he'd been out in the field, Frank had done nothing beyond transport duty and paperwork. When Mason started, he was raring to go, but they continued to suffer from "beginner's luck."

They managed not to resent each other as crap assignment upon crap assignment landed on their desks, mostly due to Frank's ability to make every job sound like the one they really wanted. These were the calls they were only following up on because they were rookies, even if they weren't called that. But Frank got excited about each one, like this one was gonna be their big break.

A few months into their partnership, Frank and Mason ended up checking out a warehouse. A neighbor in a nearby apartment building had reported suspicious characters working at night. Anyone who worked at night was, of course, suspicious, but some jobs required overnight labor. Try as they might to explain that to helpful citizens, calls about suspicious nighttime workers flooded in.

They went to the warehouse after dark. As much as most people thought there were rampant gangs of vees trolling the streets and feeding off everything that moved as soon as the sun went down, the truth was the vee population was still so much smaller than the human population that being out at night was not immediately dangerous, especially when you and your partner were armed with guns. Of course, vees had better night vision and adding cover of darkness made every mission a little less safe.

When they entered the building, Mason could tell something was odd. He'd checked out a lot of suspicious activity at night, and usually it was just humans working, but humans didn't work in the dark. From the sound of it, there was definite activity going on.

The problem with sneaking up on vees was that you can't. As soon as Mason realized there was activity, it got deadly silent. And then they were being attacked. There were six vees coming at them full speed. They weren't trying to dodge. They knew their prey's weakness in the dark.

Mason and Frank opened fire, spraying the vees with agency issued explosive bullets. Vees healed too quickly for a standard bullet to do enough harm to subdue them. Exploding bullets did more damage more quickly and your aim didn't have to be quite so dead on.

Two vees went down before they reached them. Two more tackled Frank as Mason took aim at the two headed for him. The first one didn't get a chance to touch him. The second landed on top of him, knocking him down, just before Mason blew a chunk out of his heart.

With the immediate threat to himself taken care of, Mason targeted the first vee he saw on Frank. When his head exploded, the second vee leapt towards Mason, who was already training his gun on him. He brought him down with a shot to the chest, missing his heart. The vee would live to be interrogated. More importantly, Frank would live.

By the end of that night, two vees were arrested, four more were buried, and Mason had saved his partner's life. Frank had been bitten, but not turned. Mason went from rookie status to being the guy you wanted on a hunt. Over the last three and a half years, that reputation had been earned many more times.

So when he looked back into the room, where Frank and Althea were digging around, and something caught his eye, Mason didn't hesitate.

"Down." Yelling a command worked faster than yelling something vague.

As Frank and Althea dropped down, the thing that Mason had sensed came out of the corner. He ran full speed at Frank, reaching him in seconds. Mason took aim and fired, hitting him in the shoulder, knocking him back.

The prisoner - that's what he was, one of the infected prisoners - didn't fall back or slow down. He didn't stop coming. He reached Frank and took a bite out of the closest thing he could get to, Frank's ear.

Frank shot him, point blank in the chest, and the prisoner staggered back a few steps from Frank. He looked around, taking in all his options, and charged at Althea. Althea and Mason fired continuously, bullets hitting him repeatedly in the chest, but the prisoner kept coming.

And then his face exploded. Mason had seen what an explosive bullet could do to a man's head, so wasn't surprised by the visual. The prisoner crumpled to the floor.

Frank stood up. "So, aim for the head from now on, huh?"

His face was streaked with blood. Mason asked, "You okay?"

Frank touched his ear and winced. "Eh, I'll live. Just a nibble, really."

Mason looked around the room, which seemed to be storage for blood and samples. There were freezers all up and down the walls, most with glass doors. Some held big bags of blood and some held beakers. The prisoner, when Mason had first spotted him, had been digging in a unit at the end of the room. Mason could see the empty blood bags on the floor. He'd apparently been feeding.

He looked down at the body of the prisoner. With his face pretty much shattered, Mason couldn't tell if this was the prisoner he'd seen in the hall or not. They all had the same dress code and he hadn't had time to notice any distinguishing characteristics. This could be any one of them.

The next thing he noted was that the prisoner wasn't wearing a bullet proof vest. Mason had, somewhere in the few seconds that passed during the fight, assumed that this guy had found a way to put on a vest or something. His chest was completely eaten up by bullets. Neither agent would touch the guy, not without gloves, but from looking through the exposed flesh, they could tell his organs were effectively shredded.

He looked up at Frank. "How did he keep coming?"

Frank shook his head. "That's a question for the smart people." Frank laughed to himself. "You know, the same geniuses who created this guy."

Frank was right. Cate and her colleagues had created something new. This was not a typical human. He moved too fast, withstood too much. He had qualities, in that way, like a vee, but Mason had never known a vee to survive that many bullets to the chest. You take out their heart and they die. That did the trick with pretty much every living thing. But not this thing.

He didn't know what the scientists had been trying to do here, only what they had succeeded in doing – creating a stronger, deadlier vee.

Chapter 20

Carl leaned back from the computer and smiled. Daniel's time for figuring out what Stephen was plotting was nearly up. Daniel preferred looking at it the other way, though. His time for having to deal with Stephen was nearly up. He nodded at Carl.

Carl called, "Lisa, you still here?"

Carl winked at Daniel, like he thought he'd made the world's best joke. Daniel didn't want to discourage Carl while they were in the middle of things, so he didn't shoot him. Lisa peeked out of the corner.

Carl said, "I can use that drive now."

Lisa blushed and turned her back on them.

Security for this building would not allow entry of any external storage devices. Everyone was screened upon entering the building for cell phones, hard drives, anything with an internet connection or a capacity to transport data. Carl was backing the data up to an internal drive, to take with them, but he needed something extra to corrupt the files. Lisa had been the perfect carrier.

Being pregnant, Lisa was allowed to skip the full body scans due to concerns over radiation. Instead, she got a daily pat down. Daniel had been counting on the fact that the guards would have seen Lisa every day, that they would have seen her growing bigger, and that they would've grown a little less thorough with their pat downs as the routine wore on.

To be safe, they'd had Lisa hide the jump drive in her bra. After pulling it out from the privacy of her turned back, she handed the drive to Carl, and then returned to her corner.

While Carl plugged the drive into the computer and prepared to run a virus, or whatever he was going to do to corrupt all the information he'd copied, Daniel considered their next steps, and how to deal with the other vees in the room.

Daniel wasn't worried about Joe. As someone who worked at the NVIA, Joe would know better than most the type of treatment he could expect when they found out he was a vee. If he had half a brain, he would leave this place as fast as possible and never look back. Not to mention, in his newly turned state, he probably was operating with about half a brain.

It took time to adjust to being a vee. It was like wearing a new body, at first. Daniel remembered feeling like he was hearing things, hallucinating sounds, because after the change he could hear so much more. His eyesight didn't really improve, though he knew some vees did experience enhanced vision. His sense of smell, however, increased tenfold. In a way, it was nauseating. Having a cacophony of noises assault him from all sides, and being unable to block out the sickly sweet smell of the urine left by a dog three days ago, the sweat hanging in the air of humans who'd already passed by, and the foul toxicity of everything in Kenneth's basement.

Joe would have a lot to deal with right now. He wouldn't have time to plan out some way to free his former friends or alert anyone. Besides, he'd still be weak and uncoordinated compared to the other vees. It took time to grow stronger – time and blood.

Stephen and Jerome, on the other hand, were more problematic. Daniel knew where Stephen stood - on his own – and Daniel knew how he would need to deal with him. Jerome was more of a free agent. Daniel couldn't pin him down, and that was worrisome. He figured there was no time like the present to start laying on the charm.

"Jerome." Daniel called him over to talk, called him away from Stephen and Joe. Jerome, who looked like he had nothing better to do, walked over and pulled up a chair next to Daniel.

"I wanted to get your opinion." He didn't really want Jerome's opinion, but did want Jerome to feel included.

"Okay. What's up?"

"What do you think we should do with the guards, when we go?" Daniel asked, trying hard to sound sincerely interested in Jerome's response.

Before Jerome could answer, Carl interrupted. "Done."

Daniel turned to see Carl holding up some hardware that he had gutted from the computer.

"You have everything we need on there?"

"Yup." Carl said, while putting the hard drive in the backpack Lisa had brought.

"Unlock the rest of the building doors and kill the system."

"All right. Gimme about two seconds." Carl replied, before getting back to work.

As Daniel turned back to Jerome, he saw Stephen watching. He threw him a little smile, as if nothing in the world could bother him.

He stood up as he asked Jerome again, "Well, what would you do?"

Jerome shrugged, as if it was obvious. "Kill 'em. Better not to leave witnesses."

Daniel was relieved. That's what he'd planned on doing, once he was certain he didn't need any of them alive, and he'd hopefully gotten Jerome to feel useful.

The guards seemed to know what was happening as soon as Jerome stood up. Still, just so there was no misunderstanding, Daniel announced, "Time to eat."

He loved this, the moment before a kill. He loved the smell humans got when they were afraid. The noise, not so much. Why did they always have to yell? Truly, he would take his time more often, savor the moment, if it weren't for all the damn screaming. Now that the noise had started, he felt like he needed to rush, just to shut them up.

Daniel walked over to the 5 remaining guards, with Jerome following close behind. He'd been planning on leaving one of them alive, to guide him through the building. Now they had Joe, none of the human guards were needed. Jerome knelt down to the guard farthest to the right and started eating. Daniel was about to feed on the one at his feet when he realized Stephen wasn't with them and he knew that he had made a horrible mistake. In his haste to feed, he had neglected the most important thing in the room, the guns.

As Daniel turned around, he heard Carl say, "I finished my homework Mom, can I eat now?"

Stephen was smiling at Daniel, gun aimed at his chest. Carl had stood up. Seeing the new situation, he'd frozen to the spot. Daniel smiled and shrugged, hoping by feigning nonchalance he could open a dialogue and maybe buy himself a few seconds to think.

"Oops." Daniel stated.

Jerome was oblivious, feeding. Joe was busy trying to stay conscious, barely moving in his chair. Carl, who was now alert to the situation, was about as physically adept as a manatee. No one else was going to help. This moment was between Stephen and Daniel.

"I am gonna go out on a limb here, and bet that you want to take that hard drive for yourself?" Daniel asked.

"Wow," Stephen said, with no small amount of sarcasm, "You are just as smart as they say." And then he fired.

Luckily, his aim was crappy. As Daniel launched himself out of the way, the bullets nicked his shoulder. He hit the ground hard, but had shelter behind the desks. The gun continued to fire for what seemed like a long minute. At first, Daniel thought Stephen was just wasting bullets. Then he saw that all the surviving guards had been killed.

Jerome, meanwhile, had managed to scramble out of the way, and was also ducking behind some desks. Daniel unholstered the gun he'd taken off the guard in the lab, raised his hand over the desks and started firing in Stephen's direction, hoping to kill him or slow him down.

Daniel was never so lucky. He stopped firing when it was apparent Stephen wasn't returning fire. He heard a scuffle and realized his next big mistake - not giving Carl a gun of his own. Fortunately for Carl, he was still useful. If Stephen hoped to make any money on the black market with the data Carl had just stolen, he would need him to finish the job.

"If I hear or smell you anywhere near us," Stephen called out, "I will kill him. He's not that important to me."

Daniel was still trying to think of a way out, for him and Carl. He wasn't about to risk getting his head blown off to steal a glimpse at the door. He could imagine Stephen holding a gun to Carl's head. Daniel was a great shot, but the explosive bullets these guns used affected a wider area, the better for completely destroying a vee heart before it could regenerate. If Daniel tried some sort of quick draw maneuver, he could very well rip off both their heads, and he didn't think Carl would enjoy that. He'd have to come up with a plan B.

Daniel heard Stephen say, "Sorry Joe. It's been fun." Stephen fired once more and then the door opened and closed.

Daniel risked looking over the desk then. Stephen and Carl were gone, as was the bag with the hard drive in it. All the guards were dead, including Joe. It was just him and Jerome now. He had only a vague understanding of the layout of the building, and which exits led where. How the hell was he supposed to find the server building without any guards to act as guide?

And then he heard the sniffling and remembered he had one more card to play.

Chapter 21

The final door in the long hallway was barricaded. Mason had tried to push the door open, but it wouldn't budge. The door looked worn out, if a steel door could look worn, as if someone had taken a battering ram to it.

Mason looked at Frank, who stepped forward, turned the door knob, which wasn't locked, and pushed on the door himself. Nothing happened for him either.

"Someone making a last stand?" Frank offered.

That's what Mason thought. Those prisoners didn't seem to be mentally aware enough to barricade a door, so it was most likely some of the scientists or guards locking themselves in.

If they tried to break down the door, or even tried to yell to get through to whomever might be in there, they would be making a lot of noise. Mason wasn't ready to start drawing attention. By his count, there were four prisoners on the loose and he didn't think the three of them could take them on, if they were all like the one they'd already encountered. And that was assuming they didn't have any vees to deal with.

Althea stepped forward. "There's another door. On the other side." She gestured towards the door at the end of the hall. "We could go through reception, or back around the way we came."

Mason didn't like the idea of going back. Not that it mattered, since the bad guys were mobile, and could easily be moving around the circle. At least forward felt like they were making progress.

"Or we could just leave," Frank said, stating a more practical option.

"But there are probably people locked in there." Althea insisted.

"Yeah, and they're a lot safer than we are at this point." Frank responded. "They'll just have the other door barricaded too, and they can stay, safely locked in that room, until this whole thing passes."

Mason knew Frank well enough to know he wasn't arguing out of fear. The guy hated wasting energy. And he had a point. Still, they were civilians, more or less, and Mason had a duty to make sure they were okay.

"C'mon Frank. Let's just take a peek at the other door."

Mason started moving towards reception. Frank just shook his head, like he'd expected nothing less. Althea followed behind.

As he stepped into the reception area, Mason felt immediately exposed. Beyond the receptionist desk, which was built like a mini fortress, there was an open glass wall separating them from the elevators and offices beyond. He could see a good hundred yards. Worse, he could be seen.

It didn't look like anything was moving out there, so he slowly moved into the room.

Once he cleared the desk, Mason saw the bodies. Three dead guards. Judging by uniform alone, he knew these were security guards. With how they were mutilated, he might not have recognized them even if he had known them. Mason again swept the room, making sure whoever or whatever had killed them wasn't still there.

That's when Althea walked into the room.

"Oh God." Althea ran, without caution, up to the nearest dead guard, turning his body over. She stumbled back, looking in horror at what remained of her friend, and then she crossed herself.

As Althea grieved over the first dead guard, closing his eyes and saying a prayer under her breath, Mason moved through the room. The guards looked like they'd been retreating towards the labs. That made Mason think the attackers, most likely, judging by the look of these injuries, the infected prisoners, had come out the same way he and Althea and Frank had.

Where they went after was the question.

The second dead guard was face up, though there wasn't much left of his face. Althea walked up beside Mason and stood, staring down at the faceless man, as if wondering how to make it right. There were no eyes left to close.

Mason took a handkerchief out of his back pocket. He always had one – a habit he'd picked up from his dad – though he rarely had cause to do anything with it. He laid the hanky over the guard's devastated face. Althea finally stopped staring, and looked up, grateful.

They walked together to the last dead body.

This one was different and, for a moment, Mason felt sympathy for what these men had gone through. This guard's body was intact. He hadn't been ripped apart like the others, only because he'd saved himself from that fate. It was clear from his injuries that he'd put his own gun in his mouth and fired. The monsters hadn't been interested in his flesh after it was dead. In that way, they were like vees.

Althea knelt down and closed the last guard's eyes. As much as he sympathized with her, they didn't have time for grief. Mason looked up at Frank who gave one, quick nod. Ready to move.

Mason tapped Althea on the shoulder and she stood. They all retreated back into the lab hallway, the side they hadn't been down yet. It looked clear. The door to the other side of the locked room also looked battered. Those things had tried to get in on both sides, but had apparently failed, as the door still would not budge.

Frank looked a bit like he wanted to say I told you so. Instead, he just said, "Yeah, well, we're here. We might as well knock."

Mason knew that they'd been in danger every second of this weird night, but making noise could only call attention to them. He said, "Get ready."

Althea and Frank understood. And, of course, they were both ready.

Mason knocked. There was no answer. He knocked again, a little louder, still controlled, trying not to sound like an unthinking monster beating down a door.

After still getting no response, he decided to try yelling. "Anyone alive in there?"

Nothing moved. Finally, he heard a response.

"Who's out there?"

"Agent Farino. You okay in there?"

No one answered, but Mason could hear loud scraping and banging and, after a few seconds, the door opened up.

As he suspected, the squirrely scientist, Stan, was standing in the doorway. He saw the other one standing back a few paces, holding a metal stool in his hands, as if he were prepared to tame a lion with it. When he saw who it was, he put the stool down.

"Come in. Hurry. Before those things come back." Stan, agitated and impatient, waved them in.

Mason didn't see the need to argue, though he wasn't quite prepared to be stuck in one place. When Stan tried to move forward to close the door and rebuild his barricade, Mason stopped him. Althea took watch at the door.

"We'll guard the door." Mason said, as calmly as possible, hoping to soothe Stan's nervous energy.

To his surprise, Stan laughed. "Yeah, we had a guard. There were three of them, too. I didn't see what happened, but there was a lot of screaming."

Althea looked at Stan like she wanted to strangle him. Frank shrugged with his usual authority.

For now, maybe, it would be okay to take a few minutes to gather themselves. Mason nodded. Frank patted Althea on the back, relieving her, and the two of them withdrew into the room. They reestablished the barricade, a combination of file cabinet and chair.

Mason took a moment to look around, to see if they had anything useful. Just lab stuff and computers. No weapons. There was a phone.

Mason picked up the phone and put it to his ear. Dead.

Stan said, helpfully, "Phones don't work."

Mason hung up. They'd need to call out at some point. In the meantime, he assessed the two scientists to see if either of them would be of any use in getting out of this situation alive.

Stan, he knew already, wouldn't be. He was the sort who would push you into a fight and then run over your body. The other one, James, seemed cocky and self-assured enough to want to be a hero which wasn't always a good quality, but at the moment, a hero would do well.

And then he noticed the blood. James' sleeve was torn and covered in blood.

"You injured?" Mason asked.

James looked at his arm, as if to confirm it was still there. Mason noticed the bandage under the sleeve. His wound had already been treated.

"Yeah. One of those things bit me during the fight. It's not bad though. I'll live."

Mason looked at Frank. The cut on his ear had clotted up and scabbed over already. He and Frank had survived a lot of hairy situations, and so far, they'd always managed to keep each other alive. Mason was starting to think they might even make it through this night. If they could survive until morning, he felt, unreasonably, that daylight would bring relief.

That was as far as his thoughts got, when the screaming started.

Chapter 22

As they walked up to the sixth floor, Cate, listening for trouble, kept thinking about how her career, and possibly even her life, was over. They would lock her up, or execute her, if she survived long enough to be officially dealt with.

She wasn't scared, not of her impending punishment, at least. She wanted, desperately, to be able to find out more about the pigs, and the newly vaccinated prisoners. This botched project couldn't be her legacy. Not after everything she'd done to make it here, to make a difference.

Cate guessed the vaccine had somehow made the pigs stronger, or more immune to blood-borne toxins. They hadn't died, of course. Dead was dead. She guessed that the poison running through their blood had stopped their hearts, temporarily, just long enough for them to test as dead.

She wished Stan had shared this information sooner. That, of course, was the rub. If he'd shared the information, they wouldn't have moved on to human testing.

She'd always known Stan was sleazy, but she thought he'd at least respected the basic ethics of scientific study, the code of the researcher. She wished that he cared more about science than his career. He wasn't just trying to cure the world of vees, he was trying to be the first to do it, to get all the credit.

Marisol and Cate stepped out onto the fifth floor. They were across the other side of the building from the labs where Cate worked. This was the research floor, so there were more labs on this side. It was a different department, and different departments at the NVIA weren't into sharing. Cate had no idea what they did in these labs. Probably something to do with killing or stopping vees.

This area appeared to be deserted. Cate didn't think any of these researchers had been working after dark. If they had, they weren't here now. She saw no one and, more importantly, heard no movement.

As Marisol stepped into the hallway behind Cate, she looked around nervously.

"I think it's clear," Cate said to reassure her. Marisol just held her gun more firmly towards Cate, as if she refused to be tricked.

"What are you going to do? What are you going to say, when we get there?" Cate asked.

"Listen, it's not personal." Marisol, for a moment, seemed to genuinely feel bad. "Personally, I like you a lot better than some of your co-workers, but you can't work here anymore. Whatever your motives, you are the enemy."

It was what Marisol wasn't saying that concerned her the most.

Cate asked, "And, in terms of my leaving, do you know how you want to handle that?"

"No, I don't know, not exactly. Cate, I don't want anything," here Marisol paused to choose her words more carefully, "anything unfortunate to happen to you. But this night is going to be investigated. Every detail of this night is going to be examined, and you're so much at the center of

144

this, in so many ways, that I can't see a way for what you are to remain secret. I just don't see that happening. I'm sorry."

Marisol was right. Once the vees were contained and the building was secured, there would be time to go over and over every last detail. Even without her secret, there would be much she could be blamed for. The fact that she was a vee just ensured that she would never see the light of day.

Marisol said, quietly, as if respecting Cate's thoughts, "I don't think we should stay here. I think we should get to a room with doors."

Cate laughed. It was stupid, thinking or worrying about this, when there were hordes of hungry vees lose in the building. Safety first. "Yeah. Sorry."

She turned and they started walking towards her lab. Tonight would probably be the last time she would see her office.

They walked past smaller labs. The big ones, like the area where she worked, would be on the far side of the building, behind them. These labs were for running quick tests, like processing guest blood samples.

Cate could smell the blood. They had some stored nearby and it was making her hungry. In all the excitement of the day, she hadn't had time to take lunch, to get to the refrigerators where they stored the fresh blood. She was already starving and now it seemed she might never be able to eat again.

They walked out into the lobby area, where the elevators were, and Cate stopped short.

"Wait."

Cate had a clear view into the reception area of the lab. There were bodies on the ground. She turned to Marisol and could tell from the expression on her face that she saw them too.

And then the smell hit her and she gasped.

Marisol, frightened, whispered, "What. What is it? Do you hear something?"

Cate was trying to process it. Her senses were overloading. How could that be? It was the smell of the prisoners, the vaccinated prisoners. It was coming from the direction of her lab, from the bodies, she guessed. They had the smell of rot, not like a person killed by a vee at all, but like something entirely new.

Marisol hissed emphatically, "Cate. What should we do?"

Cate couldn't bring herself to answer. There was no answer. She couldn't do anything other than look, and smell, and try to piece together the mystery.

Cate covered her nose with her sleeve and began walking towards the reception area as if entranced. Marisol hung behind until Cate had gotten almost to the doors and then she ran and caught up, sticking close.

Cate opened the glass door and the fumes almost made her pass out. The bodies smelled like carcasses in the advanced stages of decomposition. They reeked like rotten meat.

Marisol, stepping into the room, wasn't as affected by the smell. She didn't gag, just covered her mouth, and looked away. It was a brutal sight. Cate had seen worse. This wasn't personal.

Cate would never get used to the smell, but she was beginning to cope with it. As Marisol hung back, eyes averted, Cate moved towards the body on the right to start the examination.

She studied it without touching. When you didn't know what you were dealing with, it was always best to stay clean. That the guard had been bitten was obvious. By what was the question.

The bite looked like it had been made by human teeth. Vees had the same teeth pattern as humans, but vees bit the skin to get to the blood. This was different. These bites were chewed and, judging from the lack of debris on the ground, Cate guessed they were also swallowed. And, whereas a vee wound was often very clean from the ex-sanguination, these wounds looked almost gangrenous, like the flesh was melting away from the openings post mortem.

That was not supposed to happen. Dead flesh didn't continue to change. Dead was dead. As that fact sunk in, Cate had a horrible thought.

She stood up quickly, to warn Marisol. Too late. As she turned, Cate saw the other dead guard rise. He moved quickly, with the speed of a vee, and was biting down into Marisol's shoulder before Cate had time to scream.

If only she'd known about the pigs sooner, she could've prevented this. Dead was dead. This was something else.

Chapter 23

"Wow, didn't see that coming." Jerome stood up from behind the desk where he had taken shelter next to Daniel.

How had *he* not seen this coming? Daniel knew Stephen was bad news. He should've killed him when he had the chance. Instead, he'd dragged him along, let him in on his plans, all for what – because it made him feel good to have an audience? He'd let himself get careless and now everything was at stake.

"Is he gone?" Lisa started to pull herself up from the floor in the corner, where she'd been hiding long enough for everyone to forget about her. It was painful to watch her try to stand. Daniel stepped to her side, more to spare himself from having to watch and listen to her struggle, than to give her a hand.

"Thank you." She accepted his help without even cringing. She must be tired.

"Yes, he's gone, and not likely to come back."

Daniel knew exactly where Stephen was headed with Carl. He smiled to himself. Stephen was probably finding out right about now that Carl did not know exactly where to head, or, at least, not how to get there. Carl was a genius. He knew everything there was to know about computers and networks and all that kind of stuff, but he couldn't find his way out of a small closet. Daniel wasn't worried about Stephen finding the server room first, he was just hoping Stephen didn't kill Carl in frustration before they got there.

Daniel pretended to merely tolerate Carl. That was a game they'd been playing for nearly ten years now. He was a weird kid, not the type Daniel would've ever imagined being friends with, but they had become friends and he wouldn't want anything bad to happen to him. Besides, Daniel owed him.

Fifteen years ago, Daniel had still had hopes of a peaceful resolution with the humans. He was the primary face and voice of the vee lobby. It seemed like progress was being made, like the humans were considering co-habitation.

Politicians didn't want to make any official moves until they could take the temperature of their constituents. There were a lot of back room meetings and private negotiations. All the while, Daniel spoke out in public for vee rights, and politicians spoke out for stronger security to fight the vee threat. Daniel was still an optimist then. The public was divided, and he knew he only needed a few key policy makers to back his plan for integration for the country to come around.

There was one more secret meeting to attend - one more night of negotiating locations for vee reservations, guidelines for vee and human visitation, and decisions about blood farming regulations. These were real concerns and he expected a real debate. When Daniel got to the meeting, it was a trap.

Daniel was captured and locked up, and there were no witnesses. The public would think he was just gone.

They kept him alive, he guessed, so they could bring him out and show him off if needed. That was their mistake. One night, three weeks after he'd been caged, Carl showed up at his cell.   He was a pudgy 19-year-old human with a bad case of body odor.   Still, Daniel didn't receive many visitors, so he'd take what he could get.

"You here as food?" Daniel asked through the tiny hole in his door that wouldn't fit a finger let alone a juicy vein.

"Haha. You're funny."   He laughed, like it was the funniest joke he'd ever heard. Daniel thought the kid might be crazy.

Then Carl had opened the outer transfer door, a one foot square metal flap that opened onto a small opening in the wall. Daniel had a second door in his cell which would only open once the outer door was closed again. Carl put something in the chamber and closed his side.

Daniel's heart started racing the second he opened the inside door. There was a blood bag, something he sorely needed. Daniel had wondered if they'd given up feeding him. It had been nearly four days since his last meal.

Daniel bit into the bag right away, draining the contents much too quickly.

Before the kid walked away, leaving Daniel alone with his meal, he tapped on the door with his knuckle and said, "Don't forget to dispose of the bag."

A weird thing for a guard to say. Normally they left without a word. As Daniel's heartbeat slowed to a normal rate, now that he was no longer on the verge of starvation, he held the bag up towards the hole in the door. They hadn't bothered to give him a light in his cell. Vees had fantastic night vision, but it was still too dark to read in his room. As he held the bag up to the small streak of light coming in from the hallway, Daniel saw a barely legible, tiny note written on the bag in black marker. The note read, "I'm getting you out. Be ready. Destroy this bag."

Daniel had smiled to himself, not only at the prospect of being free, but because the kid had thought he needed to write "destroy this bag."

In fact, Daniel had a lot of doubts. Over the next three days - days and nights of no food, or light, or visitors - Daniel had gone over and over in his head every detail he could piece together about this young, smelly human. It hadn't left him with a lot of confidence. He was starting to think the whole thing was a psychological game introduced to torture him.

Carl had shown up on the fourth night. Through what had turned out to be a plot formulated and set almost entirely in action via back end computer programming and document forging, Carl had essentially gotten Daniel released into his custody, with no questions asked. Turns out, if you had a permission slip from the right person, federal agents would believe just about any lie.

Once Daniel was free, and he and Carl were in a safe house, Carl had asked for only one thing in return - he wanted to be a part of the vampire revolution. In a way, Carl's little request was what started the whole thing.

Now Carl was the prisoner. Daniel was certain Stephen would kill Carl, once Carl had finished with the servers. Daniel wasn't going to let that happen.

"So, you just gonna let him get away like that? I mean, is that it?" Jerome asked.

They weren't the team he'd wanted, they were the team he had. Daniel gave Lisa and Jerome his most leader-like and confident smile and said, "Nope."

Daniel grabbed spare ammunition for his gun. He got Jerome to do the same. He thought about giving Lisa a gun, but she was generally so frightened that he could see her doing something stupid and trying to make a break for it. Even a stupid gunshot wound could kill.

"Are we going after them?" Lisa wasn't looking happy at the prospect.

"In a manner of speaking." Daniel replied. "We're going where they're going, only we're going to get there first."

Beating them to the server room wasn't the problem. The problem was, Daniel had no idea what to do once they got there. Without Carl, Daniel couldn't wipe the data. Without the hard drive Carl held, Daniel wouldn't own the data. He needed Carl alive and he needed the hard drive. The key was separating Carl and the hard drive from Stephen without getting Carl killed in the process.

Daniel turned to Jerome and Lisa. "Let's all take a field trip. We're going to that little building where all the computer servers are kept." Daniel could work out the details as they walked. The one thing he knew he needed for certain was a distraction, and for that, he was going to need bait. "Lisa, be a darling and lead the way."

Chapter 24

Stan was grabbing his arm and pulling him back, as if trying to stop Mason from leaving. Althea was already clearing the cabinets away from the door, Frank helping.

Stan urged, "No. What are you doing? Are you crazy?"

Mason didn't have time to argue. The screaming from outside got louder as Althea opened the door. There was someone out there who needed his help. He pulled the arm Stan was holding sharply up, and thrust his elbow back towards Stan's chest, knocking him off and back about two feet.

As he turned away to follow Althea and Frank into the hall, Mason was caught for a second by the look of disbelief on Stan's face. It was shock, but also something else. Maybe satisfaction?

He would sort out whatever that was later. He hit the hall and saw Frank running towards reception. Mason could distinguish two separate screams – one terrified and the other angry. Both were female.

As he ran into the main room, he saw Frank and Althea with their guns drawn on what looked to be three people and a lot of blood. One of the women had stopped screaming.

"Move away from it, ma'am." Althea shouted.

The woman who was standing with her back to him, seemed to be pulling at the second person, trying to drag him off of the third. As Althea shouted, the woman turned to look in her direction and Mason realized it was Cate.

All the air left his chest as if he'd been kicked in the gut. What was she still doing here? He thought she'd left, had gotten out, long ago.

"Move!" Althea yelled.

Cate finally seemed to register what was happening and jumped back. Mason saw that what she'd actually been pulling at could no longer be called a person. It had human form, but its face was a mass of bare tissue and teeth and it was tearing at a body on the ground in the way vultures rip at a carcass.

As soon as Cate was clear, Althea opened fire. At first, the thing barely budged, but after repeated gunshots, it finally stumbled off its prey, and fell over.

Frank advanced towards the body. Mason moved closer, gun drawn.

Cate was looking between the body on the floor and the monster lying next to it. "Make sure it's dead!"

Frank moved right up to the foot of the body on the floor and fired a few more shots into the creature. Mason was close enough to see what was left of the head splatter into bits and pieces along the floor and wall.

"It's dead," Frank said proudly, as if it were him, and not Althea, who'd done most of the shooting.

Cate was still standing, locked in place, staring at the two bodies. Mason hung back. She hadn't seen him yet and he didn't want to add to her distress.

When she spoke, however, she sounded amazingly calm. "We need to be sure. These things are different from vees."

Frank looked at Cate like she didn't understand how amazing he was. "We know that. Taking the head off does the trick."

As if that was all she needed to hear, Cate ran over to the woman's body on the floor and started checking for a pulse. After a second, in which Mason assumed she confirmed that the woman was dead, Cate crumpled into a ball on the floor, hugging her knees and taking deep, gasping breaths.

He couldn't stop himself. He walked over to her and put his hand on the back of her neck. "Cate."

Her gasping ceased and she looked up at him. He'd thought she was crying, but there were no tears on her face.

"Mason."

She looked so relieved to see him, almost happy. He relaxed and realized he'd been holding his breath. She stood up and wrapped her arms around his waist, pressing her face into his chest.

If it weren't for the gun in his hand that prevented him from putting both his arms around her, Mason could've forgotten everything. For just a moment, he felt so good to have Cate back. He closed his eyes and pressed his face into her hair.

It was just a moment. Cate pulled away and looked him in the eyes. He almost thought she was going to kiss him.

Instead, she said, "Shoot her in the head."

"What?" Mason managed to ask.

Cate gestured at the dead woman on the ground. "Take her head off. Please"

"Cate. She's dead." He was trying to think of how else to explain the situation to her. What else could he say? The woman was dead.

Cate sighed, like she thought Mason was the one who was slow to grasp the situation. Then she gestured at the creature they'd just shot to death. "So was he."

Mason looked at what remained of the creature's body again. How could he have missed something so obvious? The creature was wearing a guard uniform. It didn't make any sense. The guards they'd seen here earlier were dead. Definitely dead. It wasn't possible. Of course, this had been a night of impossibilities.

As soon as he accepted that, he remembered the other dead guard. As Mason turned in the direction they'd just come from, he pushed Cate behind him, as if to shield her with his body from what he was afraid they'd find.

The body of the guard was gone.

Althea and Frank spread out and the three of them started circling the room. He couldn't keep hold of Cate and do his job, so he said, "Just stay right behind me, okay?"

She put her hand on his shoulder. He could feel her breath on his ear as she said, "Okay."

Frank said, "Room's clear."

Althea had backed up to the far wall, closest to the room they'd just come from. She said, "He must've gone down this hall, but I don't see him. How is that possible? How could he move so fast, without any of us noticing?"

"Let's get out of here. It's too open." Frank said.

Mason wanted to get Cate somewhere safe. First they needed to take care of the woman's body.

"Don't look, Cate." Cate buried her face in his back and Mason shot the dead woman until there was nothing left of her head. He turned around and faced Cate. "It's over."

She opened her eyes and he thought she might cry. Instead, she laughed, mirthlessly. "I don't think we're that lucky."

Her laugh sent a chill down his spine. Mason called to Frank, who was closest to the body dead guard who'd shot himself. "Can you grab his gun?"

Frank took the gun, checked it and tossed it to Mason. Mason held it out to Cate. "Still remember how to shoot one of these?"

She smirked. "Yeah, just like riding a bike."

He held onto it, not sure if it was the best idea, giving her the gun. Maybe he should just make sure she stayed close.

"Mason," now she looked exasperated. "I had to go through basic training like everyone else. Give me the gun."

She held out her hand and looked impatient. For a second, he felt like they were having an old argument over who got to drive. When she demanded his keys, he could never refuse. He gave her the gun. Cate disengaged the safety and held it like she did, indeed, remember how to handle the weapon.

"Guys." Frank called out. "We gotta move, now."

Mason looked over and saw three orange day glo wearing things stumbling towards them from across the lobby. He'd seen one of those things run and knew it might be seconds before they were upon them. He had no idea why they weren't already charging.

"Fall back to the room." Mason ordered.

He and Frank kept their guns on the advancing creatures while walking backwards towards the shelter of the barricaded room. Althea led the way to the door, with Cate in between.

Althea got to the door first and started knocking on it. As Mason and Frank backed up next to the two women, and the door remained closed, Althea started banging on it and yelling. "Let us in."

The prisoner creatures were still making their way across the lobby, very slowly. They were walking like drunk people and not making much progress. He didn't understand it, but Mason was glad they hadn't charged. He was afraid they wouldn't be able to take down all three of them.

"I'm sorry," came the answer from inside. "I can't do that."

Mason realized what the look Stan had given him had meant. They were locked out and he wasn't going to let them back in.

Chapter 25

Mason asked her to hold on to him. That's not exactly what he said, but Cate got to touch him more, so that's how she interpreted it. She needed something good at that moment, even if it was just pressing into her ex-almost-fiance's back as he shot her dead boss in the head to keep her from rising up and eating them all. It was the small things in life, she thought, wryly.

As Mason, the female security guard, and the other male agent - she couldn't remember his name from this morning, had that just been this morning? - swept the room, a thought popped, unbidden, into Cate's head. With Marisol dead, her secret was safe again, for now. She felt guilty for the moment of relief it gave her. Marisol deserved better. She deserved to be mourned.

Cate wouldn't be able to keep her blood type secret for long, anyway. Marisol had been right about an impending investigation. If they survived the night, and she was able to leave the building before the investigation began, Cate would have to go on the run.

Cate hadn't noticed when the one other dead guard disappeared from the room. She was still trying to get used to the idea of the dead being able to move. She was still trying to process being prey.

After Mason handed her the gun, the other agent said, "We gotta move, now."

Cate saw three prisoners in orange jump suits stumbling towards them in a semi-catatonic state. The prisoners had gotten out! That would explain why the dead guards had the same smell of rot. They must have been attacked by the prisoners, infected when they were bitten.

Cate knew these things, these monsters – she'd call them that for now - could hurt her, kill her. She'd seen how fast the one prisoner had moved to attack Andrew. He'd seemed catatonic then, as well, before he charged, and fed. After her family was killed, and she'd been turned, bitten, she'd developed an irrational fear of becoming someone's dinner. Her fear had been irrational, before, because what would eat a vee? Now, she had good reason to wonder if these things would find her tasty, which was enough to make her knees go weak.

More overwhelming though, even than her fear, was her need for answers. Why were these three not attacking already? What was causing their disorientation? Their smell? How were the original vaccinated prisoners different than the bitten guards? And how were any of them alive?

It couldn't have been more than an hour or so since she took Andrew to the ambulance. The prisoners had taken three hours to exhibit signs of change. Did the infection spread more rapidly through saliva and blood, or were the dead guards just anomalies? She needed samples to study, and time.

Cate heard Stan say through the door, "I can't do that."

She snapped back into the moment. Stan, who could've prevented this all from happening, could give her answers. The female guard banged on the door again. Was he not opening the door? Maybe he didn't understand. Cate moved forward.

"Stan, please. Let us in." Cate urged.

"Cate? Is that you?" That was good. He heard her. He knew Cate, had worked with her for years. He'd have to let them in.

"Yeah, Stan, it's a long story." Why was he taking so long? "Let us in and I can tell you about it."

The prisoners were still advancing slowly. They were near the elevators now, all three of them, bumping into each other as they moved. Disoriented and slow, yes, but they were coming closer just the same.

"I'm sorry Cate. I can't. Not with those things out there." Stan could. He just wouldn't.

Stan cared only about Stan. That hadn't changed as long as she'd known him. It wasn't going to change now. She was out of ideas and time so she looked at Mason for anything.

He said, "There's another one in there. Young, good looking guy."

James! He would help. Cate yelled, "James. James. Let us in."

James didn't answer. Stan called back. "You guys best get going. I'm not opening this door."

And then the smell hit her, hard and close, and she knew it was too late.

Chapter 26

Keeping Carl alive - and getting his hard drive back - was what Daniel really needed to figure out, and he guessed he had about ten minutes to do it. As he and Jerome followed Lisa – she said she thought she knew where the server building was – Daniel tried to come up with some sort of useful plan of attack. He could try a straightforward approach. Hide out in the room, wait for them to arrive. When Carl got to work and Stephen no longer had the gun pressed to his head - assuming he no longer had the gun pressed to his head - he and Jerome could overpower Stephen. It was the gun to the head part that worried him.

Carl had explained to Daniel why they couldn't just wipe the files in the server building remotely. The building was on the grounds of the research complex, a few yards apart from the main building. It had its own power supply, which could not be controlled from SCC. Data was automatically and regularly backed up to the servers in that building, but couldn't be accessed except in the actual room. If their plan to steal, and then delete, all the files was going to work, they'd have to wipe the data that was stored in the server room. Daniel wished Stephen hadn't overheard them talking about that. It could've saved him a lot of trouble. Of course, that was also what was keeping Carl alive.

Jerome interrupted Daniel's thoughts, stopping him on the stairway landing between floors. "Suppose I cut out when we get up there?"

So much for straightforward. Daniel had been trying to get rid of Jerome for what seemed like half the night. Now that he actually wanted Jerome to stick around and help, the guy was gonna leave.

Maybe he could be convinced. "Stephen scares you, does he?"

Jerome laughed. "Yeah, I ain't gonna take the bait. I don't care if you think I'm a coward."

Daniel had to stop assuming Jerome was an idiot. A different approach then. "Why'd you come with me? I mean, why didn't you leave sooner?"

Jerome shrugged. "I don't know. Thought you might have a big idea or something."

Ah. This was familiar ground. Ideas were something Daniel was good at. "I do, and that hasn't changed."

Jerome didn't seem that impressed. Lisa got to the landing above them and sat down to wait.

Daniel insisted, "Listen, Stephen is going to try to take that list and sell it to the highest bidder. Who do you think has the biggest need for a list of every known vee and their whereabouts? Who do you think wants that list more than me?"

Jerome rolled his eyes at the obviousness of the answer. "The humans. Government, probably."

"Exactly. And when they get it, they will go right back to rounding us up, experimenting on us and exterminating us."

"Yeah, well, I don't plan on going back to my old hangouts anyway."

Jerome didn't seem to understand exactly how important this was. Daniel pushed on. "I can stop them. Not only will they not know where to find us, but I'll be able to contact every vee out there. I can lead us to a new world order."

If they could leave here with the only copy of the biggest compiled list of vee whereabouts in existence, it would take the humans years to recover. It would only take Daniel weeks to set in motion the next part of his plan.

"Yeah, you know," Jerome said, sounding a little embarrassed, "I appreciate what you're trying to do and all, but I think I just want to live to eat another day, you know?"

Daniel smiled at Jerome as if it wasn't the least bit of a problem. "Completely understand." And then he went back to thinking Jerome was an idiot.

There would be no convincing him. Daniel had no more time to waste. He walked away from Jerome, up the stairs and offered Lisa his hand. "Allow me."

Lisa looked startled, but took his hand. Since she was his only ally at this point, albeit only because he was holding her husband hostage, still, since she was with him through thick or thin tonight, he might as well be nice.

Jerome caught up. "This is G? Yeah, here's where I get off."

Before stepping past Lisa and Daniel and opening the door out into the hall, Jerome asked Lisa, "Can you point me towards the nearest exit?"

"Oh, okay." Lisa opened the door and stepped through, with Jerome beside her. Daniel followed, but as soon as he stepped into the corridor, he knew by the smell that something was wrong.

Lisa said, "It's real easy. You just go down here until you come to another hallway, and then turn left. That's if you want to get to the main entrance," Lisa paused for a moment, like she was remembering what was at the main entrance and thinking of an alternative. "Oh, but I guess that would be fine."

They were standing in a long hallway. This building had a lot of long hallways. Daniel looked both ways, but didn't see anything. Still, the smell was disturbing.

"You smell that?" Jerome crinkled his nose.

Daniel turned to Lisa, "Time to go."

He put his hand on the stairwell doorknob..

She looked confused. "We're on the ground floor. We just have to walk to that end of the building, and then outside."

The smell was getting stronger, fast. Jerome started turning this way and that, trying to track down the source.

Out of time. It was here.

Daniel put his arm around Lisa's shoulders, pushed open the door to the stairwell, and pulled her in. As soon as he did, he felt a rush of air and heard a yell as something knocked Jerome to the ground.

Daniel hissed, "Run." Lisa still stood there, as if not understanding what was going on. "Run." He pushed her towards the stairs and she started running up.

Daniel planned to follow her in a second. This was Jerome's fight, he wasn't going to help. He just wanted to see how it played out. Daniel peered through the window on the now closed door. There was a man dressed in prison orange wrestling with Jerome. Jerome was yelling and trying to push him off, but the man was winning!

How was that possible? Jerome was bigger than the prisoner. Daniel knew the prisoner was no longer human, he could smell the change on him. It seemed to him that the prisoner was stronger than human, like a vee. Only, not exactly.

Jerome was fighting for his life – trying to stay alive. This thing didn't seem to care. It was focused on feeding, not on surviving. It didn't seem to mind the blows that Jerome landed on him. And since Jerome wasn't using his teeth, he wasn't slowing the thing down at all.

As Daniel turned to follow Lisa up the stairs, he saw the man bite into Jerome's arm. No, not bite. That wasn't the right word for it. Vees bit. This thing had ripped.

Chapter 27

There were only a few shots fired before the dead, faceless, rotting, guard charged down the hallway and into Althea. She fell down on top of Cate, and their three bodies knocked Mason and Frank back a foot towards the lobby.

In the two seconds it took Mason to recover, the thing had started chewing on a chunk of Althea's cheek. She was screaming and trying to free herself. She and Cate were pinned beneath it.

Mason saw Frank take aim with his gun at the creature's head. "No!" The bullets could kill Althea, or Cate. "We need to knock it off her."

Mason started to move to do just that when Cate yelled out. "Behind you!"

He turned to see two of the formerly slow and disoriented prisoners charging towards them. Frank turned as well and they both started firing. The things were moving too quickly for targeting the head. Mason shot the easier target of their bodies, trying to slow them down. They were coming fast.

And then his clip was empty. He didn't have a spare. He hadn't thought he'd need one for a routine transfer job. Frank wasn't going to be able to hold them off for long and they were penned in from all sides. If he could get that thing off of Cate and Althea, get Althea's gun, and get Cate free, they all might have a chance.

As Mason turned back towards Cate and Althea, the head of the creature on top of the two women exploded. Mason threw his arm over his face to protect it from the bullet shrapnel, and the blood. It was over as fast as he'd reacted. When he looked down again, Cate, who had somehow gotten her gun free, was holding it in her one hand and trying to use her free arm to push the dead creature off of her and Althea.

Mason pulled the body off. Althea's face was a bloody mess, but she was still alive. He could hear her crying. Her eyes were clamped shut and the tears weren't making any streams in the thick cover of blood.

Cate stood up and stepped next to Frank, firing at the charging prisoners. Mason leaned into Althea's still intact ear. "I'm gonna take your gun and get you out of here."

She nodded and released her gun into his hand. While keeping hold of the gun, Mason got his arms under Althea's, propped her up, rotated her and started backing down the hall.

"Let's move." He called, so Frank and Cate would know to retreat.

It was clear Stan wouldn't be opening the door now. Mason started dragging Althea to the next door down.

"Goddam it!" Frank holstered his gun, turned to Mason and said, "I'm out."

They were barely holding back the attack as it was. Not a good time to ease up. Mason stepped forward to fill Frank's position. "Take over." He nodded towards Althea.

As Frank turned to move, he yelled, "Look out. Hallway."

Mason swung his gun around, facing the other direction. The third prisoner was coming towards them down the hall. Mason couldn't help thinking it had circled around on purpose, to surround them. Could it have thought that through?

Frank started pulling Althea while Mason advanced in front of him down the hall. He looked back towards Cate, to make sure she was holding her own, to make sure she was all right. She would need help soon. He just needed to get them a few more feet to safety.

The prisoner at the far end of the hall was still moving slowly, groggily. Mason saved his bullets. There weren't enough to spare and this one wasn't a good enough target, yet.

He turned back just in time to see Cate stumble and fall backwards, tripping over Althea's feet. The two prisoners were upon them in a second. Both latched onto Althea. Cate was free beside her, so Mason leaned over Frank, grabbed Cate's arm and pulled her back and away from the things with as much force as he could muster. She practically flew towards him, and they both stumbled to the ground next to Frank.

"Get into the room." He insisted to Cate.

The two things were attacking Althea's legs, her thighs. She was screaming again, begging. "Help me. Help me!"

Cate stumbled over Mason and headed towards the door.

Frank was pulling on Althea, trying to hold on, but parts of her legs were being ripped away.

Mason started shooting over Frank's head, trying to aim high enough not to hurt Althea, but low enough to do some damage. He couldn't get a clear shot at their heads with Frank in the way.

Mason pulled Frank off Althea and Frank, weaponless, ran for the door. The prisoners, distracted, perhaps, by the movement, stopped feeding and looked up at Mason as if anticipating their next meal. Mason started to back away, slowly, like you would with a rabid dog. No quick movements.

He looked behind him. The door was open. Frank had made it inside. That other prisoner, the one who'd circled around, had stopped walking now. It was staring at him too, and it was only about ten yards away.

Althea was still repeating, "Help. Help me." Her voice was barely a whisper.

Mason was going to kill those things. He took aim. The two on top of Althea first, then the other one.

"Mason, back, now!" Frank shouted.

Mason turned in time to see the third creature charging. Mason broke and ran. He practically dove into the room. As he turned back towards the hall, Cate and Frank were already closing the door behind him.

"Wait." Mason ordered.

The third creature had joined the other two, digging into Althea's outstretched arm. Mason quickly took aim and fired. As he collapsed back into the room, Cate and Frank slamming the door closed, he was just thankful that Althea's head had been an easy target to hit.

Chapter 28

As Cate stood there, back against the door, those creatures banging into it, she hated herself more than she had ever hated herself before. She could've helped that woman. She could've saved Marisol. If she'd acted faster. She was thinking slowly, responding even more slowly, and people were dying because of it.

Mason yelled "Move." She did and he tipped a file cabinet into the door. Then she had to move again as he knocked another one over.

"Other side." Mason gestured and the other agent moved to the door at the far side of the room.

They were in the observation deck. Everything was dark. The emergency lighting in the hall was bright enough for people to find their way around. In this room, there was just enough light to keep a human from walking into the wall.

The creatures kept banging on the door they'd just come through. It wasn't giving. Mason watched as the other agent maneuvered two file cabinets in front of the far door.

"You okay?" Mason asked.

Cate muttered, "I never even got her name." She knew she was being maudlin, but she didn't care.

Those things terrified her. When she'd been pinned beneath him, and his teeth were coming towards her, she could hear the skin being ripped off. She could smell the disease on his breath. She wasn't afraid of death. If she died, she wouldn't have to feel anything anymore. But those things didn't promise death. As frightened as she was of being chewed on, she was most afraid of being turned into one of those monsters, of being responsible for killing more people, seemingly without care.

"Cate, everything happened very quickly." Mason put his hand on her shoulder, as if to comfort her. "You couldn't have done anything more."

"That should do it." The other agent walked up to them. "My name's Frank, by the way."

He held out his hand and smiled and it was so ridiculous Cate had to laugh. "Cate. Nice to meet you, I guess, under the circumstances and all."

"Yeah, lovely place you got here. Great ambience."

Cate smiled at him. "It's seen better days."

"Yeah, you know what's nice? Ireland. You should go there one day."

"Frank, don't start that again." Mason griped.

Frank sat down and leaned up against the wall, under the two way mirror. "I don't know about you guys, but I'm thinking we just sleep here and wait until the cavalry arrives."

Mason squinted at Frank. "You okay? Looking kind of shabby."

Frank shrugged and said, "I've been up for, what, twenty hours? I'm tired."

Cate could sympathize. This had been the second hardest day in her life. She wished it was over already. She wished Mason would take his hand off her shoulder and wrap her up in his arms and make this night go away.

"You want to tell us what those things are?" Mason asked.

Oh God. If only she knew.

"I don't know what they are." She shook her head in frustration. "A few hours ago, they were human."

Mason took his hand back. "Well, you have to know something. Why don't they die? Why do they move like that? What did you guys give them?"

She could try to explain. "It's top secret, of course."

Frank laughed, "Yeah, I think the secret's out."

That was true. This night had taken them beyond security clearance into need-to-know. "We gave them a vaccine. It was supposed to be a vaccine against vampire infection. When I started here, that's what our goal was. A sort of sterilization project." That had been a lifetime ago. That had been many lives ago.

Cate continued, "The drug we were working on turned out to be lethal to vees. In testing, a vee ingesting the vaccinated blood died, which opened a door to eradicating the vampire race."

"Jesus, Cate!" Mason spat. "You were okay with that?"

"They killed my whole family, Mason. You know that. They left me with nothing. I hate them. I do want them dead. They don't deserve to be alive when everyone I care about is dead!"

Mason turned his back on her, and she knew she'd hurt him. She hadn't meant to. She wanted to add, "Except you. I care about you." But she still couldn't say that.

Mason turned back and glared at her. "So, it didn't work, huh? You tried to get rid of one race and instead you created something worse. What are they?"

That was the question she'd been asking herself. "They're humans that we injected with an experimental attenuated vaccine." She stopped, and forced herself to continue in English. "The vaccine we injected was made with a live, but weakened, version of the virus that causes vampirism. At least, that's what the original six prisoners are – infected humans. The others..."

Frank asked, "Why do they move like that?"

"It would seem that their blood has merged with the serum we injected and become a mutated form of vee blood. They're fast and strong because of that. I can only guess the other, semi-catatonic state, is because they're newly changed and haven't adapted yet. And some of them were grievously injured before turning. The good news is they don't seem to heal like vees."

"Yeah, or die like vees either." Mason was quick to point out the bad news.

"They die." Frank piped in. "Just gotta take their heads off."

Cate went on. "The others, the guards, were infected by the prisoners. I'm guessing when they were," it didn't seem an adequate word, "bitten. They didn't die, actually. I mean, I think they had started to change, before their human body stopped functioning."

"So, you fail at curing vampirism and instead you create zombies!" Mason spat out, accusingly.

"They aren't zombies." Cate responded, weakly.

"Really?" Mason prodded. "You have a better word for it?"

She wanted to laugh. Zombies. But she was a vampire. And now the dead were coming back to life.

"Hey, mom and dad, hate to interrupt and all," Frank didn't sound like he minded one bit, "but do you hear that?"

Mason stopped talking but continued to glare at her. Cate looked away, focused on listening for what Frank had heard. She didn't hear anything. She didn't hear any noise at all.

Chapter 29

Daniel could have abandoned her. She was human, and slow. She was pregnant, and even slower. He could've left her to die, but he might still need her.

They ran up two flights of stairs until they stepped out onto a floor. Daniel hated to admit it, even to himself, but that thing was scary. It had taken down Jerome, a much larger vee, without too much of a fight. He supposed if he'd stayed and helped Jerome, they both could have defeated it. The thought hadn't even crossed his mind. What did that say about the kind of vee he was?

"Why did that vee attack?" Lisa hadn't seen what had happened to Jerome, not as much as he had.

"That wasn't a vee." Daniel wasn't in the mood to talk.

"It looked like a vee, I mean, it moved fast."

"Yeah, unlike you," Daniel thought to himself.

Explaining - what little he could explain - would just freak her out. Calm Lisa was better than screaming Lisa, even if she was slower to move.

"He was one of the inmates, wasn't he? A volunteer?" Lisa seemed intent to not let it drop.

"Yes, he was one of your friends' experiments. When he volunteered, I'm sure he didn't know he was going to end up being turned into, whatever the hell they turned him into."

Lisa asked, "They turned him into that?" She really didn't know.

"Yes. They gave the prisoners some drug that made them different." Daniel continued, voice and anger rising, "As I said before, the NVIA doesn't seem to care about the impact their experiments have on vees, or apparently on humans either. They act as if the ends justify the means."

Lisa looked abashed. Daniel hadn't meant to get upset. He started off again in the direction they'd been heading. "We are still walking in the right direction, yes?"

Lisa looked around. "Yes, I suppose we are."

She didn't know? The woman was just walking at random? He needed her to focus. There was a trap he needed to spring, as soon as he could come up with it.

Lisa collapsed against the wall and started taking long, deep breaths.

"Oh God, don't tell me you're going into labor?"

She didn't bother to answer for a minute. She seemed to be losing her fear of him. Maybe he'd have to do something about that.

"I'm sorry. I think that was a contraction." She held up her hand, reassuringly. "Just a contraction. You can have them for days before the baby comes."

She leaned on the wall, like it was holding her up. "I just need a minute."

She didn't look like she'd be ready again in a minute. Daniel was about to push her, maybe even to frighten her into moving, but he imagined it must be hard, carrying all that extra weight around. Still, he was in a bit of a rush.

Daniel looked around and his eyes actually spotted something that could help. "Come with me."

She looked at him wearily, but followed.

He couldn't believe it, but the sign was true. There was a fitness center on this floor, just past the stairs they'd come up. These people killed for a living. They destroyed families and friendships. They tortured. All in a day's work. And then, apparently, they worked out?

It was a smallish gym lined with mirrors and filled with barbells and treadmills and other fun, sporting activities. After looking around the room for a second, Daniel saw what he was after.

"Sit." He ordered, and then added, "Please. We'll move again in a minute."

Lisa sat down on a weight bench. Daniel picked up a twenty pound weighted barbell, walked over to the vending machines against the wall, and smashed them both open. He grabbed a bottle of blue energy drink and a few packets of crackers and brought them back to Lisa. She actually smiled.

"No chocolate?" she asked.

He smiled too. And then he got the lady a chocolate bar.

He sat down next to her as she started to eat.

"Thanks for this." She talked at his reflection in the mirror to save herself from turning around. "I thought I was going to faint."

"Yeah, that's what I was afraid of." That hadn't even occurred to him. That really happened?

He looked at himself in the mirror. He didn't look like he'd aged another fifty years in the last two hours, even though he certainly felt that way.

Lisa stopped eating for a second. "Was that true? What you said back there? About Stephen and the highest bidder?"

Unfortunately it was. "Yes. I've known people like Stephen before." She was listening like she cared, so he went on. "Not willing to do their own work. Completely willing to steal someone else's." He couldn't keep the hatred out of his voice. "No interest in building a better future, in fixing what's broken. It's all about the now. And always, always, out for number one and number one only."

"And you? What are you out for?" Food had made her braver.

"I'm trying to save my people from your people." He stood up. This conversation had taken too long.

Lisa stood up, faced him, and said, "I'm sorry."

"For what?"

"For my people." As Lisa walked out in front of him, Daniel had a sneaking feeling it wouldn't be so easy to use her as bait after all.

He needed an edge. He looked at his reflection one more time, forcing himself to think of something. His reflection smiled back. At least one of them had just come up with a plan.

Chapter 30

"What are they doing?"

The zombies - she would call them that until they had a better name - the zombies had stopped trying to break in. Or at least they'd stopped charging the door. Mason and Cate and Frank all sat still, listening. Cate could still smell them, but she wasn't sure if that was because they were still there or if it was just their foulness hanging in the air.

"Maybe they left." Frank suggested.

"Shhh." She cut Frank off. She heard something. What was that?

Thack!

Cate screamed as a zombie smashed into the two way mirror. She grabbed Mason's hand and backed up. "They're trying to break through the glass." Could they do that?

Mason held her hand. He sounded much too calm for the situation. "There's only one. His body is still just human. He can't smash through bullet proof glass." He smiled as if to say, just one, harmless little zombie. "I guess he's just noticed us."

Cate was annoyed with herself that Mason talking to her as if she were a child afraid of the dark actually did calm her. Still, she was relieved that he was taking a softer tone with her. She had enough stress at the moment.

She was holding the hand of a man she'd walked away from, never offering him the explanation he deserved, while staring at a monster she helped create who could very well kill all of them before the night was out. She felt her guilt trying to rip her gut open. If only she could figure out a way to undo some of the damage.

Thack!

This zombie looked human. He'd apparently been in the same room all night and had no injuries, so there were no rotted wounds to make him appear frightening. But his behavior sent chills down her spine, especially since she knew that he was capable of killing her and the others. She wasn't sure if he was trying to climb the mirror or trying to scratch it away. The zombie was clawing at the glass, which wasn't the most disturbing part. What finally made her look away was that he kept licking and chomping at the glass, as if there were a tasty meal waiting for him, just beyond his grasp.

Mason squeezed her hand, "You okay?"

She smiled back at him, "No." And then, realizing there might not be another chance, she said, "could we, maybe, have a talk?"

He shrugged. "Sure."

They walked to the far side of the room, only 50 feet or so from Frank, but it gave them all a little privacy, and Cate felt better not being directly next to the zombie show. They sat down across from each other, knees touching. Silly, how much something like her knee cap grazing against his reverberated throughout her body.

"Before you start in about the zombies or whatever," Mason laughed a little, like he was saying something ridiculous, and then continued. "I need to know, Cate, why wouldn't you call me back? Why wouldn't you see me?"

How to explain not showing up to the funeral, not taking his calls, disappearing with nothing more than a final text telling him to leave her alone. There was no explanation that would convey the enormity of what she'd done. No explanation but one.

"Mason, I…" she started, but he cut her off.

"I know you blame me for not being there. I know you think none of this would've happened if I had just gone with you, like we'd talked about. I'm so sorry, Cate. I am so sorry about your family."

"No. No." He couldn't have thought that. All this time. "No, Mason, I never blamed you. Oh God, I'm so sorry. I couldn't face you because I had changed. I never thought it was your fault for a second. Please. Please, forgive me."

And then he was kissing her and she was kissing him back and it was the happiest Cate had felt in five years. For a moment, they weren't trapped in a room, trying to survive. It was just his lips, pressed against hers, his arms around her waist, his tongue testing hers.

She let the kiss go on too long. Despite all the vees in the world and the zombies at their door and the stink in the air. Cate let Mason kiss her. Cate kissed Mason. And she held on to that moment like it was the last happy moment she'd ever have, because it probably would be.

Mason broke the kiss and said, "I have never stopped loving you. I tried. And I still expect answers, but…" It was exactly what Cate wanted to hear, but she had to tell him now, or she never would. Before she could respond, Mason continued. "I needed you to know that, before I leave. Just in case."

Her heart stopped. "Leave? To go where?"

"We have to warn the outside about the zombies. Who knows how many there are at this point, since they can make new ones. I need to get to my car to make a call. Get this place shut down."

Cate said, "It already is."

She told him about trying to leave the building, about the slaughter, about everything she'd seen before coming back here. Maybe that was enough, to keep him with her. Maybe he would stay now.

He looked like he wanted to hug her again. He looked like he wanted to punch someone. Then he just looked tired. "The escaped vees must have gone to SCC, to lock the doors remotely."

Mason looked beyond her. He looked at Frank. "You ready to get back to killing vees?"

Frank groaned and toppled over.

Chapter 31

"I'm not going anywhere." Frank sounded exhausted, or like he had the flu. Mason hadn't thought he was as tired as all that.

Mason said, "If you need to stay..." Frank wouldn't back out of a mission unless he really had to.

Cate gasped. "Oh." And covered her mouth.

Frank smiled at her, like they were sharing a joke. But Mason could tell it wasn't funny.

He looked at Cate, who looked like she'd just seen a puppy hit by a car, and back to Frank, who looked like he'd just been hit by a car, and then Mason understood.

"No. No, Frank. It was just a little scratch."

Frank chuckled. Or maybe it was a sob. Mason couldn't tell, as the smile never left Frank's face.

"That's what I thought too. I really didn't think about it at all, until the two of you started talking about bites and infections and then I figured maybe I'm not so much tired as... something else."

Cate knelt down next to Frank, took his arm, and helped him sit up again. "I'm so sorry. I didn't know you'd been bitten."

There had to be something they could do. Mason asked, "Can you give him an injection, or something? Maybe some other vaccine?"

Cate looked up at Mason. There was no hope in her eyes. "I don't know. If we could get to the blood supply, across the hall. Maybe an infusion. We could try to flush it out."

She sounded like she was reaching. He didn't care. "Right, just across the hall. What else would you need? Just blood? Are there needles and tubes and all that over there?"

Frank started coughing. "Uh, I don't feel so good."

He didn't look so good either. When had he gotten so pale? Even in the red glow of the room, he looked like death. There was no time to waste.

Mason said, "Hold on. I'll be right back." He started to move the file cabinet.

"Stop!" Frank hissed.

Frank held his hand out to him. What was he doing? Wasting time. Mason went and took Frank's hand. He was shocked by how cold it was.

"You can't leave me alone with her." Frank insisted. "I don't want you coming back in here finding out that I had your girlfriend for dinner. You'd never forgive me."

Mason said, "Shut up. Nothing like that is gonna happen."

"Sit down." Frank ordered. Mason sat down next to Frank, opposite Cate. Frank looked suddenly pale and clammy. This was happening too fast.

"Listen," Frank was no longer smiling. "I don't want you wasting time or risking your life for something that won't help anyway."

"We don't know that." Mason insisted. He looked over at Cate. She shook her head, as if she thought it was already too late.

Frank looked like it took every drop of energy he had to keep talking. "I just shit myself. Okay? And that was bad enough. I don't know how long we have. I need you to end this before I turn into one of those things."

"Frank, I can't do that." He couldn't. How could he kill his friend?

"Yes, you can and you will. I'm done arguing. Tell Susan..." Frank broke off. Mason wanted to look away. He couldn't bear to watch his friend cry.

"Shit. Just make something up for me." Frank nodded, like he was ready. Mason wasn't ready though. How was he supposed to do this?

He looked at Cate. She was crying, but she nodded at him in understanding. She always could read his mind. He knew what to do now.

Mason mustered a smile for Frank. He didn't let go of his hand. He looked him right in the eyes and said, "Just one more time, tell me about that honeymoon of yours."

Frank laughed. Mason was glad that he got him to laugh, because then Frank didn't notice Cate pulling the trigger.

Chapter 32

Daniel knew the idea was stupid and probably wouldn't work. Today had been a long day, and this evening had gone not quite according to his perfect plans. He was about plum out of anything original and brilliant.

"Turn it to the left a little." He shifted it a smidge and Lisa said, "Perfect."

Daniel walked out from the aisle of servers and took Lisa's place by the door. "Would you stand over there for me?" he asked.

She walked back over to where he'd been. Perfect. From where he stood in the doorway, if he stared at where she actually was, he couldn't see her at all. She was blocked by a row of servers. If he looked straight ahead, like someone who'd just opened the door, Lisa's reflection in the mirror appeared just like she was straight in front of him.

The illusion wouldn't last for more than a second. Daniel had to assume that would be enough time. At least, that's what he hoped.

He let the door close behind him and walked back over to Lisa. He handed her his gun.

She took the gun as if it were a very expensive and breakable teacup. "You remember how to use one of these?"

Lisa glared at him for a second, but she started holding the gun like a gun, so he didn't mind. Daniel was about to walk away when she stopped him.

"Miguel?" Lisa asked. "Is he really okay?"

"You're husband is fine. You'll see him again soon." Daniel smiled in what he hoped was a believable and reassuring manner. Lisa was looking nerve-wrackingly uncertain. Daniel added, "I think it's best we get in position. No telling when they'll arrive."

She looked nervous. "I really don't feel comfortable with this. What if I hit your friend?"

Now that she'd stopped sniveling all the time, and had indeed proven useful, Daniel was beginning to like Lisa. When this night was over, he might even help her and her husband escape the area, if that didn't prove to be too inconvenient.

Daniel reassured her. "Carl will be fine. Aim low and if you nick him in the process, serves him right."

Daniel led Lisa over to the end of the aisle where she was going to hide until the action started. He gave her a "you can do it" hard stare. She smiled. As he walked back to his position, facing the mirror, he hoped she could. He hoped she didn't kill Carl. That would really screw up his plans. He was willing to take that risk. Had no choice, really. Besides, Carl had cushion. It would take a lot of bullets to get through all that flesh.

He rubbed his forehead to try to get the tension out. This part of the plan was supposed to have been the easy part. Now, Daniel had to sit here and wait and hope that his friend didn't end up dead, that Stephen did, and that he was able to leave with a big fat backpack filled with the only copy of the NVIA data base. Was that too much to hope for?

Chapter 33

The last thing Cate wanted was to leave this room, putting the two of them in danger, but Mason was going to remember he wanted to leave sooner or later, and maybe getting him on mission again would be a distraction from his loss.

"Let's get going." Cate stood up, and held her hand out to help Mason. "We have some people to warn."

Mason snapped his head up and looked at her so quickly, she thought she'd scared him.

"Cate! Your friend, James." Mason looked horror stricken. "He was bitten!"

Cate was getting used to the sinking feeling in the pit of her stomach. That meant… "Stan."

Mason stood, put both hands on her shoulders and looked her dead in the eye. "You ready for this?"

She smiled at him, as much to assure him as to lie to herself. Ready to face an army of zombies and possible death by digestion? "Sure."

She took one final look at the zombie locked in the prisoner room. He was still trying to eat through the glass as mindlessly as ever. She could sympathize. She was pretty hungry herself.

Mason checked her gun and his own for bullets. "We don't have a lot to go around, so only shoot when you have a shot. Got it?"

"Got it."

She trained her gun on the door while he moved the file cabinets. The door didn't instantly spring open with zombies rushing in, which meant they were going to live a lot longer than she thought they would.

Cate made it to her office door unmolested. She didn't smell any zombies, beyond the odor that hung in the air. Mason nodded at her, signaling the all clear. Apparently special agents in the field didn't use words.

She knocked on the door. "Stan. It's me, Cate."

"Cate?" She was shocked he was still alive. He sounded relieved to hear her voice. "Cate, I still can't let you in."

Cate pressed on, through her irritation. "Stan, listen to me. You have to get out of there. You need to get away from James."

Stan sighed loudly. "James is dead, Cate, and I'm not opening this door."

Cate took a deep breath. She could smell it now. It was stronger. There was a zombie somewhere close. Out of time, again.

"Stan, I know about the pigs. Marisol told me before she died."

"I don't know what she said, but it wasn't true." Stan lied.

How did he get to be her boss when he was such an idiot? The smell. She looked past Mason but didn't see anything.

"I don't care, Stan. Listen to me, this vaccine does something, makes it so infected people don't die. They come back to life, Stan. Like the pigs. James isn't dead, he's…" What to call it? "He's mid change. You need to get out of there before he gets up."

She heard movement behind the door. Good. Not too much of an idiot. He was finally listening.

"Cate, I can't move the file myself." Stan said, panic sneaking into his voice.

Cate could only imagine how the cabinet was propped, having not seen it, but she had a pretty good idea how physics worked. "Climb under it and kick it off the door."

Cate wished he'd hurry. The smell was so strong. It had to be right there, but she couldn't see anything. It was as if the zombie was right on top of her. She couldn't see it, but it had to be…

"Stan!" Cate yelled, desperately. "Get out of there. Now."

She heard him rustling around. "I'm trying." He whined.

She tried the doorknob. Locked. "Unlock the door, Stan." Cate started pushing on the door, even though she knew it couldn't help. "Unlock the door. I can help."

Too late. Stan began to shriek.

Cate backed as far away from the door as she could, all the way to the wall. She couldn't take her eyes off the doorknob, as she covered her ears. She couldn't drown out Stan's screaming. The noise dug into her and became the only thing - Stan's shrieks of pain behind the door that wouldn't open. Cate couldn't blink. She couldn't move. The screaming went on forever and she was trapped by it.

Mason stepped in front of her, forcing her to look at him. "Cate." He said calmly. And she heard him. "Cate. We have to go."

And then Cate was able to move again, because the screaming had stopped.

Chapter 34

Mason led Cate quickly away from her office. Stan had stopped screaming, which meant that James, or what had been James, would start looking for his next meal soon.

As they stepped into the stairwell, Cate grabbed his arm. She was staring off in the distance, blankly. "Andrew had a cell phone."

"What?" Mason asked.

She looked at him and then her eyes seemed to come back into focus. "Andrew. His cell phone. There are cell phones in the lobby. We can call out."

Of course. They didn't need to go all the way to SCC for a phone. If they could get to the lobby, get hold of a confiscated cell phone, he could warn his director about what was going on. Keep the building locked down. Keep those things from getting out.

Slowly, he and Cate made their way to the ground floor. Somehow, they got to the lobby without seeing a vee or a zombie.

What he saw there more than made up for having arrived unscathed. The entire room was littered with dead bodies. He'd never seen so many in one place before. There must be eighty people, dead. Cate was unfazed. Of course, she'd been here when the slaughter had started. Mason, on the other hand, had to remind himself to breathe again.

Like so many things he'd seen that night, there was no time to process. The storage lockers were near the guard desk by the building's main doors. He didn't want Cate to have to walk through the minefield of blood and death. Not again.

"Stay here." He said. "I'll be right back."

As Mason made his way across the lobby, trying to find areas of floor to step on so as not to walk on the corpses, he realized two of the front doors were propped open by bodies. He headed there instead of to the lockers.

The six bodies jammed in between the two sets of doors were dead guards, in full body armor. These weren't the guards from the front desk. They looked like they were from an exterior guard patrol. Mason guessed they'd come to investigate the alarm, seen the bodies in the lobby, and entered the building. The worst part was that these guards must've been killed by zombies, judging from their injuries. There was no telling if some dead guards had already risen and walked out into the night. There was no way to know if, or when, these corpses would reanimate. There was no telling where the zombies who killed them had gone.

Despite the implications, the doors being opened had one positive effect.

Mason called out, "We can get out, Cate. I have a phone in the car."

Cate looked frozen in place. Horror stricken. Mason wasn't sure if she was in shock from the carnage, or if it was something else. "Cate?" Mason asked.

One of the dead guards sat up about two feet away from him. Cate must've seen the zombie moving before even he had. Fortunately, the zombie had not focused on anything yet. Mason was sure it would sense food nearby soon enough.

No point in trying to make it outside now, not with Cate on the wrong side of a field of bodies, and both of them stuck on the far side of the soon to be walking dead. Chances were that the others would wake up shortly and they didn't have enough bullets to kill them all. No time to try to break into a locker, either.

"Cate." He whispered. "Get ready."

He started walking slowly towards her, careful not to trip on legs or arms. Carefully, he watched his step, and watched Cate. He saw her eyes widen in terror.

"Mason." Cate shouted. "Mason. Run."

Chapter 35

As the door opened, Daniel prepared to give the performance of his life.

Stephen pushed Carl into the room in front of him, gun stuck in his back. After taking a couple steps, Stephen saw Daniel and just shook his head, as if in disbelief.

Stephen said, "I didn't think you'd be that stupid."

Time to start the show. "Whoa, whoa." Arms open in front, acting the supplicant. "I'm unarmed."

Stephen pointed the gun at him. "Very stupid." And fired.

That happened a lot faster than Daniel had anticipated. He hadn't gotten to use half the speech he'd prepared.

The mirror shattered into a million pieces. Stephen stopped firing, obviously stunned for a second, but it wouldn't last long. Where was Lisa? Why hadn't she fired yet? If she chickened out or changed her mind, this whole thing fell apart.

And then there were more gunshots, coming from Lisa's direction.

In the few seconds he was distracted, Daniel charged at Stephen. As he moved, he saw Carl fall to the ground. No time to worry if he was okay. He better be okay.

Stephen began firing back at Lisa. Daniel leapt into him, knocking him over. He tried to wrestle the gun away from him, but only managed to knock it out of Stephen's hand. The gun skittered across the floor. Guess he was going to have to kill him the old fashioned way.

Daniel tried to rip Stephen's throat out with his teeth. Stephen was no longer unprepared, though. He was in the fight, and he was stronger than Daniel.

Stephen held Daniel's shoulders, keeping him away from his throat. That was okay with Daniel. It kept Stephen's hands occupied. Daniel's were free to reach into his pocket and bring out plan b.

Before Daniel was able to grab what he was looking for, however, Stephen knocked Daniel to the floor, climbed on top and straddled him. Daniel put his free hand on Stephen's chest, grabbing a handful of shirt, trying to hold Stephen off his neck, but Stephen wasn't interested in biting. Stephen was reaching for his gun.

For whatever reason, neither Carl nor Lisa was coming to his rescue. Daniel needed to get his hand free of his pocket before Stephen could reach his weapon. He took a risk and let go of Stephen's shirt.

Stephen fell off of him, recovered almost immediately, grabbed his gun and was turning to fire when Daniel shoved the shard of mirror into Stephen's heart. He twisted and pulled out, and plunged the makeshift knife in again for good measure. Stephen's face grew pale rapidly. He looked surprised as his eyes froze over in death.

Daniel scrambled out from under Stephen's legs and crawled over to Carl. After everything they'd gone through, Carl had to be alive. Daniel turned Carl's body over, face up, and Carl opened his eyes, slowly, as if scared to see who it was.

Seeing Daniel, Carl was smiled. "Hey, you won!" He sat up as if nothing was wrong.

"You're not shot?" Daniel asked.

"Me? No, why would you think that?" He saw the look on Daniel's face and then seemed to understand. "Oh, yeah, figured it would be best if I played dead."

Daniel would make Carl pay for this, later. For now, they had some servers to destroy.

"Get to work." He ordered.

All in all, not a bad plan. Everything had worked out nicely.

Carl started operating a touch screen monitor attached to the first row of servers. Daniel had time to breathe, and to look around.

Lisa was lying prone against the far wall. He could only see her legs and the bottom of her dress. And the blood. He could see the pool of blood she was lying in.

Chapter 36

Mason knew enough not to look back. He continued to run as he got to Cate, grabbed her arm and pulled her towards the stairwell. Mason threw open the door and they stumbled in, him pulling the door closed behind them. They weren't exactly safe, but there was a door at his back and he could take a second to come up with the next thought.

They couldn't go back up. There were too many zombies up there. At least, he hoped they were still up there. They couldn't leave. The main exit was swarming with zombies and they were almost out of bullets. They could try another exit. Once outside, they'd still have to head for the main gate, and that meant back towards the zombies. And since he hadn't been able to get a cell phone, there was no way to call for help.

Except there was. The emergency phone in SCC would have power. There was a chance the vees who took over the building were still there. Mason would rather fight vees than zombies any day.

As Mason started to move forward, away from the door, Cate grabbed his arm and stopped him, pushing him back a little ways behind her. He followed her gaze to the landing just half a flight up. James was standing there, eyes fixated on Cate. He swayed as he stood, and his mouth hung open, as if trying to taste her through the air.

Mason wasted no time. He took aim and fired.

Only James hadn't waited. He'd run down the stairs so fast, he seemed to have taken the flight in one jump.

Cate slammed back against the door so hard, she and James bounced and fell forward onto the floor, with Cate on top. Thankfully, the blow hadn't knocked her out and as soon as they landed, she pushed off of James, falling to the side.

Cate clear, Mason fired again. His first shot took off a chunk of James' skull. It wasn't enough to stop James from jumping up and charging Mason.

Mason fired again, hitting James in the chest, but it didn't slow him down. James knocked into Mason and they fell backwards, landing near the edge of the steps.

James snapped at his face. Mason had managed to brace his arm between them, keeping James' teeth from reaching his face. His arm wouldn't hold him off for long though. Mason rocked his body up and launched to the side, throwing James off of him and down the stairs. He'd used too much force and found himself rolling down the steps after. He tried to catch hold, to break his fall, but he only managed to slow it. Somewhere in the fall he lost the gun.

Mason came to a stop halfway down the stairs and started to scramble back up, to get to the gun. He felt a hand around his ankle and looked back just in time to see James pulling. Mason was jerked backwards, falling out and down, and landing hard against the floor.

Mason must have blacked out because it seemed like he blinked and James was on top of him, but Cate was there too. She had her arm around James' neck and she was trying to wrestle James off of him.

"Cate." He managed to say, despite the weight on his chest. "The gun."

She pulled away and he didn't see her for a second. James snapped at him, hadn't stopped snapping at him, and Mason was afraid he wouldn't be able to hold him off any longer. Then he felt a gun being pressed into his hand.

"Stand back." He put the gun in James's mouth and opened fire. Mason closed his mouth and his eyes as the blood went everywhere. What remained of James landed on his chest.

Mason pushed the body off of him and stood up. Cate grabbed him and hugged him. "Mason, are you okay? Tell me you're okay."

"Yes, Cate. I'm fine." He squeezed her tight, as he apologized under his breath. "We have to get out of here."

As he pushed Cate in front of him, towards the stairs in the direction of SCC, Mason pulled his shirt sleeve down, covering the bite mark.

Chapter 37

There was a dead guard in the hall outside an open door. Cate had never actually been to SCC, but Mason stopped in front of the room like they'd reached their destination.

She hadn't smelled anything rank on the walk down here, well, rank beyond the normal rot of dead, still human bodies. She hadn't smelled any zombies, and didn't now. She also didn't hear any movement anywhere around them, but she waited, dutifully, by the corner across the hall, while Mason moved in to check the room.

He came out a moment later and gestured her in. She joined Mason in the room and he closed the door behind her, locking it with a dead bolt. They weren't even going to have to build a barricade this time. They could be safe here, while waiting for help.

Mason picked up a phone in a big red box and dialed, just like that. He started speaking into it, saying his name and his ID number and getting through all the security type stuff Cate assumed was necessary for a call like this. In the meantime, Cate looked around.

The room wouldn't have been comfortable on a normal night. The dead guards strung up in the back made the room downright eerie. From the look of it, most of the guards had been shot, but there were at least two with vee bites, and one who'd been bitten and shot. What had the vees been up to?

Cate watched Mason give his report. She felt like this was the end, like the night was over and they'd made it and she could let go of all her fear and just wait for Mason to sit down beside her and hold her until the sun came up.

"I believe some may have already fled the perimeter." Mason stated flatly. "I don't know how many. There were six to begin with, but we saw at least six others who looked like they'd been infected by the first batch."

He looked over at Cate, right at that moment and she thought, "He knows." But he only smiled at her, as if reassuring her. She was being silly. If he knew, he would've left her by now.

Then Cate remembered something she had forgotten for what felt like a million years, and had actually only been a few hours.

"Andrew." Cate said, almost a whisper. Then, more firmly, "Mason, Andrew got taken to Fairfax Hospital."

Poor Andrew. He was the best of them. She only hoped he'd died quickly and not turned into a zee, though she knew that was improbable. Her entire team was gone. Cate once again found herself the last one left alive.

Mason relayed the information to his boss. Cate could only imagine how his report must sound. She supposed they dealt with a lot of unbelievable realities as Special Agents.

Mason continued, "I can only assume all of the imprisoned vees were freed by someone working within the NVIA. Also, it looks like the computers are down here. They might've done something to them, or it could just be from the power going out."

Cate looked around. All these monitors would normally have stuff on them, she supposed. The room was well-lit, seemingly with full power. That made sense. You'd want your security to be up and running, even during an emergency, though it hadn't done much good in this case.

"Sir, I have a woman with me, Cate McCready." Cate's ears pricked and she looked over at Mason and smiled. He turned his back on her and lowered his voice. She could still hear him just fine though.

"If the team gets here, to SCC, and anything has happened to me, let them know she's here. She's a scientist who works in the building and I brought her here to protect her."

What was he talking about? What could happen to him now? He wasn't planning to leave again? She wouldn't let him leave her.

She stared at the back of his head, waiting while he finished his call. Finally, he hung up, turned around, saw her watching him and smiled at her, like they'd just won a prize. "The cavalry is on their way!"

She didn't return his smile. "What was that about? What could happen to you, Mason?"

Mason frowned. "You weren't supposed to hear that."

Cate wouldn't be deterred. "You can't leave. We're staying here. We're safe here."

She almost started to cry. To have made it this far, with him, she wouldn't let anything else happen. They had survived. He had to stay with her. He had to.

He walked up to her and kissed her. As much as she wanted to melt into him, to let the kiss happen, she pushed him away. What was he trying to do? Placate her?

"Mason, what? What is it you're not telling me?"

He looked into her eyes, all attempts at a smile gone. "I'm sorry Cate. I was hoping we could have a little more time before you had to find out."

She shook her head, backing slowly away. She didn't want to know anymore. She felt a scream building in her throat. She wanted him to stop, but it was too late. Mason rolled up his sleeve. He'd been bitten. She was too late. She was alive. He would die, or worse. There was nothing she could do to save him. She felt so helpless - useless. How could she be expected to sit here and watch him die? But what else could she do?

And then she did start to cry.

Chapter 38

Daniel leaned over Lisa's body. She was alive, though, from the amount of blood pooling around her, gurgling out of the bullet holes in her chest, she didn't have long.

She opened her eyes and looked at him. He sat down next to her and took her hand.

She spoke in a whisper. "My husband? Is Miguel really alive?"

"Yes. Well, that's how I left him." She closed her eyes as if she was fighting back tears and Daniel decided it might not be the best time for humor. "I left him safe. I swear."

"Thank you." She wheezed, but didn't open her eyes again.

Daniel felt guilt. He'd planned on her surviving, or, at least, that he wouldn't be responsible for her death. He didn't exactly care about her, so much as he didn't dislike her, and this was his fault. She'd been shot while trying to help him.

Lisa propped herself up on her elbow, opening her eyes. She was about to say something when she started coughing, and choking, as if blood were caught in her throat. Daniel was uncomfortable. Strange. He didn't like to see her suffer. Daniel sat her up, hoping to ease her discomfort a little.

There was one thing he could do, to make himself feel better, to help with the guilt. He had to act fast for it to have any chance of working. When Lisa stopped coughing, Daniel said, "I'm going to turn you. You can survive."

Her eyes went wide and she squeezed his hand hard. "No! No. You'll kill the baby."

Was she stupid? The baby would die when she died. He was offering to save her life. "You can have another baby."

She just glared at him and he realized, of course, that no, she couldn't. Maybe she didn't understand what was happening. "You'll die."

She collapsed into him, her head lolled over onto his shoulder. She grabbed onto the collar of his shirt and sputtered, "Take the baby to my husband."

Now that had to be a joke. Was she crazy?

She didn't seem like she was joking. "Swear to me. Swear to me that you will take her out of me and get her safely to my husband."

"I can save your life." If he hurried, before she bled out, he could. "Just let me help you."

"Please. Swear to me." She wasn't going to let him off the hook that easily. "Swear to me you'll take her and keep her safe. Please."

Realizing what she meant to do, Daniel was moved. Sympathy wasn't something he was used to having. Nor was respect. What else could he do? "I swear."

"Thank you." Lisa started to cry. "I was looking forward to meeting her. I wish I could hold her, just once."

She was sobbing and all Daniel could do was rub her back and keep her from falling over. He found himself wishing there was a way to fix this.

Maybe just some encouraging words. "I'll take care of her. Your daughter will be safe."

Lisa stopped crying enough to take in a ragged breath. "I don't know how long we have." She looked scared, but determined. "You better do it now."

This wasn't going to be easy.

Daniel laid Lisa down and ran past Carl, who was typing away, oblivious to everything around him. Daniel had no idea which piece of the broken mirror would be the best for performing an emergency C-section, so he grabbed a few that looked like they would make good knives.

Lisa had lost so much blood, he was surprised she was still conscious. He wished that she weren't, as this was going to hurt.

Daniel took off his shirt and wrapped it around his hand, making it easier to hold the mirror shard. He leaned over and whispered to Lisa, "I'm ready."

She cracked open her eyes. "Not too deep. Be careful. Please."

He placed his free hand on her forehead. It was cold. "It'll be okay. She will be okay. I promise." Lisa didn't respond. She just closed her eyes. "Get ready."

As he cut into her belly, Lisa screamed and arched up before passing out.

Daniel was glad she'd passed out, because he was making a mess of it. Trying to cut a person open, with a piece of glass, while trying to be careful not to cut too deep, was complicated. He had to slice through layers of skin and muscle too, before her belly opened up and he could see the baby inside.

It was amazing. There was a little baby in there, all snug and safe. Daniel was able to pull her right out. He wiped the goop off of her as best he could and she started crying immediately.

Daniel laid the baby on Lisa's arm, her little body pressed up against Lisa's chest, her face up to her mother's face. He'd seen this maneuver in a million movies and, as Lisa was still breathing, he thought it might be best to put the baby with her mother. Daniel shook Lisa, trying to rouse her.

Lisa opened her eyes. He hoped she saw her baby girl. He thought she maybe even smiled a little, as she gasped her last breath and her eyes froze over.

Daniel cut the umbilical cord and tied it in a knot. It wasn't pretty, but he hoped it would do. He wrapped his shirt around the baby, and held the little girl in his arms. She actually stopped crying and fell asleep. When she was lying quietly like that, Daniel could see why so many people liked babies.

Carl walked up to the two of them. "Aww, man, you got a baby?"

Daniel looked at Carl, who was looking at the baby like she was the cutest thing he'd ever seen. Sometimes it was hard to believe Carl was a genius. He wasn't much, but he was what Daniel had to work with. Everyone had to start somewhere.

"You done over there?" Daniel tilted his head towards the servers.

Carl looked up in surprise, like he'd forgotten the whole reason they were there. "What? Oh, yeah, good to go."

He walked to the exit and held the door open. Carl stepped out of the building.

"Hey. You gonna get that?"

Daniel pointed at the backpack Carl had left behind, the bag that held everything they needed, the hard drive with all the information they'd come here for. Carl had walked right past the bag, like he and Daniel hadn't nearly died for it tonight.

Carl snorted, "Oh, yeah. Sorry."

Carl picked up the backpack and slung it over his shoulder. Daniel held the baby close to his chest as they walked out into the night together. If Carl was what he had to work with, Carl would have to do. Everyone had to start somewhere. Daniel started with Carl. Soon, though, he'd have an army to work with. Wouldn't that be something?

Chapter 39

Cate choked back her tears. Mason. No. She couldn't let him die. Cate wouldn't watch another person she loved die. It was as simple as that. He couldn't die. She wouldn't let him.

Mason just kept talking, as if trying to snap her back to the present. "I won't make you do it. I'll leave. You won't even have to see it happen. For now, I just want to be with you, while we have time."

"No." He looked like she'd slapped him in the face. "No. I won't let you die."

"Oh, Cate." He looked at her sympathetically, like he was going to have to spell it out for her.

She was the one who had to do the explaining. And more, she was the one who had to do the apologizing, now that she knew how to save him, or at least, how she was going to try. But it had to happen quickly. There was no time to be gentle.

"Mason, sit down with me." She led him over to a corner of the room where there were no dead bodies and where there was a wall to lean against. Mason followed, but he still had that look on his face, like she was going to need his help. "Mason, please, sit down." She said, more firmly.

He sat down next to her. She decided to start with the most important thing. "I want you to know that I love you."

He smiled, relieved, like this was what he'd been hoping for. "I love you, too."

She put her hand on his shoulder, keeping him from leaning forward to kiss her. There wasn't time.

"Mason, I cannot live with you dying." It was true. She'd barely survived watching her family die. She'd only managed by not allowing herself to feel anything.

"Cate."

"Don't interrupt. We don't have the time. I want you to understand that it wasn't by choice that I left you. It was because I knew you'd never forgive what I had become. I need you to say that you forgive me. I need to know that you will forgive me."

"Of course." Mason said, earnestly. "Of course, I forgive you."

"Promise me you'll forgive me everything." Cate knew she was playing a dirty trick. At this point, she deserved a little bit of peace, even if she had to trick him to get it.

"Cate, I love you." She was about to go on, but he took her hand and said, "And I know."

She wasn't expecting that. "Know? Know what?"

Mason sighed. "That you're a vee. You gave it away a few times tonight. And knowing that, I finally understood. Took me long enough." He smiled, wryly.

If only she'd known five years ago that he would forgive her even this. There was no time for regret now. No time for anything but action.

"Thank you." She said, and smiled with relief.

And then, Cate bit him. She sank her teeth into his wrist, into the foul wound the zombie had made, and she drank.

Mason screamed, and tried to pull his arm away. He tried to push her off of him. She was stronger. She held him and kept drinking.

She looked up at Mason as she drank, as he came to fully understand what she'd been asking him to forgive. He fell back against the wall, shaking his head, tears in his eyes. "Cate. Please. No."

She didn't know if she could really save him, but she hoped by draining most of the blood out of him, like sucking the venom from a snake wound, she could get rid of the infection. As she ingested the zombie blood, she thought, it didn't hurt. She'd been so afraid it was going to hurt. Mostly, the blood just tasted bad. Like sour milk.

Mason started to weaken. She saw his face turn pale. She saw his body slacken. The blood had started to taste normal again. She hoped that meant she got it all. There was nothing more she could do.

Cate stopped drinking and released his wrist. Mason was still conscious, but barely.

Cate hadn't actually witnessed a vee drink infected blood – they'd never managed to study that - and this was a new variable. She couldn't know exactly what would happen, or how long it would take for her to die, assuming that was the outcome. Ingesting human blood that had been tainted from a bite by an infected person would undoubtedly have a different effect than injecting the virus directly into a pig, or a vee, or a human, for that matter. She would soon find out. Her final experiment.

"I'm sorry. I couldn't tell you." A feeble apology for the past five years, but it was all she could muster. "I knew you'd never be able to look at me again, the way you had when I was human."

"I would've loved you no matter what." Mason squeezed her hand. He looked at her like he was the saddest person alive. He looked at her like he was about to lose the person he loved most in the world. She realized she was leaving him again. A selfish thing to do. She left him because she wasn't strong enough to watch him die.

Cate crawled over Mason's legs, and leaned against the wall next to him. She put her hand against his cheek and he pressed his face into her palm. He was still warm, despite the blood loss.

"And do you love me still? Even now?" Cate asked, needing to hear it.

"I will love you forever, Cate."

She felt so warm inside. She thought, at first, that it was happiness, burning a hole in her heart, melting away the years of pain. Then the warmth turned to fire and she realized her blood was boiling. The infected blood was spreading.

"Mason." She moaned. "It hurts."

He pulled her into him, cradling her in his arms. "Cate, what can I do?"

Nothing would stop the pain, now. Nothing could make it go away. There was one thing she wanted to do before she died.

"Press your lips to mine, and hold me close."

And he did. Cate wished she could feel his kiss. All she felt was the pain filling her entire body. She wanted to scream, but she wouldn't hurt Mason like that, wouldn't leave him with that memory. She kissed him back, as if it were the best moment in her life, as if she weren't in pain. She wanted him to have that, at least.

As the pain built inside her, she started to lose consciousness. She welcomed the darkness, but struggled to open her eyes, one final time. She looked at Mason, kissing her, and imagined that moment at the airport, back before the nightmare began.

She closed her eyes at last and returned to her memory. Cate was standing at the airport, before any of this had happened. She was kissing her boyfriend goodbye, knowing that she and Mason would see each other again soon, knowing that they were going to continue their life together, that they would both be so happy with each other.

Mason kissed Cate once on each eyelid and said goodbye and then it was over.

Epilogue

As Daniel walked into the Arlington house they'd been using as a home base for the past year, the sun was shining. It was going to be a beautiful day.

Carl followed him in carrying the baby. After a short tussle, which Daniel had lost primarily to give his ears some rest, he'd let Carl take over baby safety. Daniel had held onto the backpack. It was more important to him anyway.

As they descended into the basement, Daniel was nervous. It must be the exhaustion, because apprehension was something he simply never felt. He didn't want to see Lisa's husband just yet. He wanted to sleep first. Recover. And then get to work. Thanks to the baby, they didn't have that luxury. She was going to need milk, and diapers. There was no way he was letting Carl focus on all of that when they had a revolution to start.

Miguel, Lisa's husband, was loosely tied by his ankles and wrists to an easy chair in their finished basement, watching TV. Not the worst prison they could've kept him in.

Nicole, one of Daniel's small and soon to be rapidly growing army, stood up when she heard them enter. "You did it?!" He smiled. She ran up to him and hugged him. "I knew you would."

It was a scene of domestic bliss, except for the man tied up in the chair. Except for the baby of his dead wife sleeping in Carl's arms.

"Go upstairs." Daniel commanded. "Tell the others. Send Eric down."

She saw Carl, and the baby, and shot Daniel a questioning look. He shook his head. He wasn't ready to explain. Not to her.

Once Nicole had left the room, Daniel walked to the front of Miguel's chair, bent down, and started untying his ankles.

Miguel, realizing for the first time that Daniel had returned, said. "Where's Lisa? She obviously helped you or you wouldn't be here. What did you do with her?"

Daniel didn't answer. He finished the ankle knots and then untied Miguel's wrists.

As soon as he was free, Miguel shot up to standing and yelled in Daniel's face. "Where's my wife?"

In response, the baby started to cry. Miguel turned to Carl in disbelief. Carl walked forward and tilted the baby up, giving Miguel a good view of her. As Carl rocked and shushed her, the baby's cry quieted.

"She's perfect." Miguel spoke in awe. He made a move to take the baby, but Carl turned, slightly away from him and he stopped short. He turned to Daniel and demanded, "Where's Lisa?"

Daniel stated, "She's dead." He fully expected Miguel to strike him. It's what he would've done. He anticipated retaliation. Yelling. Something.

At first, Miguel just stared at him open mouthed, as if trying to decipher a phrase in a foreign language. Then he turned to look at his daughter with renewed intensity, still silent. The silence lasted a millennia. Finally. "Will you be releasing us?"

Daniel gestured towards Eric, who'd made his way downstairs. "He'll take you both home or to the hospital, whichever you prefer. You'll have to be blindfolded, of course."

Daniel was beginning to think this wasn't going to be as bad as he'd feared, until Miguel spoke again. His voice broke. "How did she die?"

Daniel had survived a lot worse things in his life than an awkward conversation. Still, he wanted to share all the gory details of Lisa's death with Miguel about as much as he wanted to drink sour blood. He did it, though. He even managed to make it sound a little less gruesome than it had actually been.

At the end, mostly because he thought it sounded right, Daniel said, "I'm sorry for your loss."

Daniel gestured and Carl handed the baby to Miguel. Eric signaled for Miguel to go up the stairs ahead of him. Before taking a step, Miguel, holding his daughter tight, glared at Daniel with such pure hatred that Daniel was sure this man would find a way to kill him.

Miguel laughed, mirthlessly. "You will never be forgiven for this."

Miguel started to walk upstairs with Eric, but Daniel, feeling he still owed something to Lisa's memory said, "You and your daughter should leave the area. Today, if possible. It won't be safe here anymore, for humans."

Stupid, to have said anything. Miguel would tell the NVIA agents everything he could. With that, and what they were going to find at the research facility, they might be able to piece together some understanding of what he had in mind. Of course, by the time anyone figured out his plan, it would be too late.

Acknowledgments:

It takes a village to raise a book. There are really too many people to thank and I apologize now for the many, many people I won't get to mention by name who have leant their thoughts or other forms of aid to me while I worked on this novel.

Thank you to Bart Robinson for the cover design and making the website look as dashing as you do! And, of course, thank you for all of the other love and support you give on a daily basis.

Mary Supley Foxworth couldn't have done more to help with the writing and launching of this book if she'd tried. In fact, I imagine she tried! My sincere gratitude for all you do for me and my career and my dreams.

You don't get a lot of love as an unknown writer – for your writing. For encouraging me to keep up the good work I have to thank the first person who ever supported my writing financially. Thank you to David Furst. We'll always have Metro Connection.

On that note, I have to thank the storytellers and fans of Better Said Than Done for continuing to contribute to and support the art of true, personal storytelling, and by extension, me.

And here are some of the brave and patient people who have given me notes, comments, and criticism over the years. You know I love your feedback, even if I don't always listen. Thanks to: Richard Barr, Barbara deBoinville, Joanne Lozar Glenn, Peter Gorman, Chris Greenlee, Cathy Hostetler, Jerry Kalke, Len Kruger, Mary Lucas, Pamela Potter, Kimberly Ruff, Katie Spurlock, and Jeremy Strozer.

And for general writing related insight and encouragement: Paula Adkins-Boyland, Stacy Crickmer, Freddi Donner, Mel Harkrader Pine, Urmilla Khanna, Lisa Leibow, Anne Loehr, Meredith Maslich, Jayne Raparelli, and Paula Whitacre.

About the Author:

JP Robinson is a writer, performer and video producer. JP's writing includes a myriad of formats, from radio commentary to hour-long storytelling shows, and screenplays to novels. JP is a storyteller with and the founder of Better Said Than Done, Northern Virginia's premiere storytelling troupe. After graduating from NYU's Tisch School of the Arts with a BFA in Film and TV Production, JP launched Capture Video, Inc., a corporate video production company. JP has been a regular commentator on WAMU, DC's NPR station. Publications include the true, personal story, "The Game," in *Sucker for Love*, and, "What Are the Odds?" in *The Northern Virginia Review*, Volume 29.

www.ingramcontent.com/pod-product-compliance
Lightning Source LLC
Chambersburg PA
CBHW070621130626
46556CB00001B/435